Crafted Murder:
A Medium with a Heart

Book 5

Erica J Whelton

Publisher: Sunseri Design Publishing
ISBN: 978-1-956069-14-3

Printed in the United States of America

To my Aunts Mary, Evelyn, Rosalyn, and Angela. Thanks for being like second moms to me and always supporting my dreams.

Books in this series:

Premedicated Murder (book 1)
Replicated Murder (book 2)
Organized Murder (book 3)
Inherited Murder (book 4)
Crafted Murder (book 5)
Destined Murder (book 6)

Other books by this Author:

Mandy's Story: Courage – Finding Herself Series (book 1)
Becca's Story: Purpose (book 2)
Caroline's Story: Serenity – Finding Herself Series (book 3)

The Haunting of Anna-Rose (Paranormal Suspense)
Decoding Us (Women's Fiction/Friendship)

<u>Coming in 2024: New Culinary Cozy</u>
Appetizers and Alibis: Alphabet Soup Mysteries (Book 1)
Biscuits and Bodies: Alphabet Soup Mysteries (Book 2)
Cornbread and Coffins: Alphabet Soup Mysteries (Book 3)

Chapter One

It was early Saturday morning, and I was watching my adoptive daughter, Oakley, and rescue mutt, Chewy, playing together in the living room. They were playing their favorite game that involved Oakley throwing the ball and Chewy chasing it and bringing it back to her.

He would gently drop it at her feet, causing a deep belly laugh from her before she'd scoop it up and the game would start again. Though occasionally, he would run around with it and not let her have it, which only caused her to laugh harder as she chased behind him, yelling his name, or at least her version of his name.

He was so gentle with her; I was thankful for that. I'd really been blessed with a good dog.

I had the news on in the background, hoping to catch the weather report. We'd had a few rainy days, but we had plans to meet my friend, Laney Landon, and her daughter Aspen at the park later today, and I didn't want to get caught in the rain.

I'd met Laney when I investigated her late husband's murder. Jeremy Landon was the father of both Oakley, my adopted daughter, and Laney's daughter, Aspen. The whole situation had been a nightmare. Jeremy's pregnant mistress, Cate, had murdered three people, kidnapped me, and then went into labor while holding me captive.

When I shared that story with others, they looked at me like I had two heads. I understood because I had moments when I couldn't believe this was my life either.

Laney had been pregnant at the same time, and oddly enough, had Aspen just days after Oakley was born. They were half-sisters born only days apart. Our plan was to raise them knowing each other.

It was nearly their first birthdays, so we decided it would be fun to celebrate together. If they were okay with sharing, we wanted to do it for their entire lives.

Today we were meeting them to let the girls play, and the moms were going to finalize the party plans. We were both planners, so we worked well together.

I turned my attention back to the television as the reporter announced that the weather was all clear for the day.

"So, if you have outdoor plans, enjoy the sunshine." The meteorologist smiled at the camera.

"Great! Should be a fun day." I grabbed the remote to switch off the television when the breaking news story caught my attention. I stood listening with my finger on the power button.

"There was a death today at Birdsong Senior Living. The victim is said to be an eighty-year-old male. Initial report is a heart attack after a brief illness. Foul play is not suspected." The reporter paused, and then she smiled. "In other news, the zoo has a new baby elephant."

The report continued, but I switched it off.

"Why are they reporting the death if no foul play is suspected? I would imagine it was old age, right?" I said to Chewy, who had walked into the kitchen to see if I had any food.

His big doggy smile always made me melt, so I tossed a treat from his bag. He snatched it from the air, then trotted over to rejoin Oakley for their game.

I quickly finished packing.

"Snacks? Check. Extra diapers? Check. Extra clothes, sippy cup? Check and check." I shouldered the bag and my purse, then grabbed my keys. "Alright, little girl, want to go see Sissy?"

She giggled and quickly toddled to the front door.

"Go. Go." She banged on the door.

"Yes, we'll go." I looked at Chewy. "Sorry, buddy, not this time. We'll be back soon."

He wagged his tail but didn't make a move to follow us. He was a good boy.

As we drove over, I played the children's songs she loved and listened to her try to sing along. It was adorable. We had gone to Mommy and Me music classes for about six months now. We both enjoyed it, so we kept going.

She loved the other children, the singing and dancing. I think it was, in part, why she started walking early. She wanted so badly to dance with the other older children.

When we arrived at the park, I saw Laney and Aspen getting out of their car. I pulled into a spot near them.

"Hey, Jo!" Laney greeted as she strapped a wiggly Aspen into her stroller. Aspen was pointing at Oakley.

I unbuckled Oakley from her car seat, then settled her into her stroller so we could follow our friends. We started out by walking the nature trail around the pond, chatting casually, while the girls jabbered back and forth, occasionally reaching for each other.

"Their friendship is so sweet. I'm so glad we can get them together like this." Laney said.

"Me too. I'm also glad that Nina's baby turned out to be Butch's, and not Jeremy's. That would have been awkward to have another sibling out there."

"So true."

We stopped to let the girls watch the ducks waddle around and swim in the water.

"Dawg?" Oakley asked.

"Wuack?" Aspen replied.

"It's a duck," Laney and I said in almost unison.

They clapped and giggled as they watched them a moment more before we continued our walk. We made our way around the pond back to the swings and got the girls out, putting them each into one. They started giggling.

"So, you promised you'd tell me what happened with you and Clint," Laney said.

"Uh, I don't even know where to start."

"At the proposal, obviously. What did he say, and why did you say no?"

"Well, you know we'd just solved the case with the Senator, and he just got caught up in it." I sighed. "He didn't want to marry me. It was just excitement, adrenaline that had him blurt it out."

"Did he say that?"

"No, I mean not exactly, but why else would he just blurt it out?" I threw up my hands. "We'd never talked about it. Not one conversation about our future. It was always casual. Well, casual-ish."

"But y'all seemed so happy."

"Happy doesn't automatically mean we should get married."

"Well, that's true. So, is that it then? You broke up?"

"Kind of. I mean, I asked for a break to think, some space."

"But you also said no, so what do you think he's thinking

now?"

I shrugged. We hadn't talked since that day. It had been about a week. I had no idea when we'd talk or even if we would talk again. My heart ached at that because I loved him, but I wasn't ready for marriage.

"Yeah, good point. I honestly don't know what he thinks, but I had dated Ted for several years and look how that turned out. He'd been living that double life, and if he hadn't been killed, I would have never known."

"True."

We were quiet for a while as we continued to push the girls on the swings. They giggled and chatted to each other, enjoying their sister time.

"Your grandmother still lives at Birdsong, right?" I asked.

"Yeah, she loves it. They have a lot of fun activities. She plays bingo and cards weekly. Once a month, they have movie nights. There are two dining rooms, plus a bistro. I've had lunch with her a few times, and the food's all great. Your dad will love that."

"Sounds nice." I giggled. She knew my dad too well. He loved food. "Since my dad's fall, I've been trying to push them towards moving there."

Not a lie, exactly, because I wanted them to move there. However, I also wanted an excuse to research Jack and maybe have a look around for clues.

"I'd be happy to give y'all a tour if you'd like."

"That would be great. It might help me sell it to them."

"I'll call Gramma later and ask her when we can come visit. She loves showing off Aspen to her friends and frenemies alike."

"Frenemies?" I laughed.

"Oh, yeah, there's always drama around there." She chuckled.

"Drama? About what?"

"There are more women than men, so there's competition amongst the ladies. The men are like kings and can pick and choose who they date. Often dating more than one at a time." She winked.

"I can only imagine what that must be like." I wondered if that was why Jack said he had no enemies and that everyone loved him. "Do you know Jack Reynolds?"

"The guy that died this morning?"

"Yeah, I saw it on the news. Just curious if you might have met him when visiting your grandmother."

"Only casually. I don't think Gramma was friends with him exactly." She giggled. "She says she has no interest in men, or women for that matter. She's happy being herself and alone. But yeah, I had met him a few times. Like I said, more women than men, and that one had a big personality."

"I hope I have her attitude when I'm that age."

I'd met her grandmother twice. She was a sweet and spunky lady and had been quite the fox in her day. Heck, she still was.

Aspen started yawning.

"Well, we need to get home for lunch and nap," Laney said.

"Yeah, us too."

We loaded up the girls and walked back to our cars. As I turned to say goodbye, I remembered.

"Oh, we didn't talk about the party."

"Darn. Oh well, we have everything handled, right?"

"Yeah, I think we do." I grinned. "All my guests have RSVP'd yes. You?"

"All but my Aunt Carol. She's out of town."

"I'll be there early so we can get everything set up."

"Perfect. I'll call you later."

We hugged, then each climbed into our cars and left. I thought about Clint and his proposal. It helped me process it a bit to talk it out with Laney.

I didn't have an answer or any idea when I might see him again. It wasn't on the top of my list of things to do.

We arrived home. I carried a sleeping Oakley into her bed. Chewy was so happy to see us. He spun around and around as I carried his friend to her bed. She would likely sleep another fifteen or twenty minutes, which gave me time to relax before I fixed us both lunch.

I let Chewy into the yard and switched on the television. It was the lunchtime news. They were once again reporting about that death at Birdsong.

Did they always report on deaths there, or was I just paying attention because I wanted my parents to move there?

Chewy came trotting in and sat at my feet, leaning into my leg for some head scratches.

"If this was just an age-related death, why are they reporting it?" I said as I rubbed his ears. He drooled a bit. "You love me."

A deep voice interrupted my conversation with my dog.

"They're lying, you know. I was murdered."

Startled, I jumped nearly out of the chair. My reaction caused Chewy to bark. I spun around to look for the source of my fear. There stood a spirit.

"Oh, um, hi. You're..." I pointed towards the television. "The victim?"

"I am, and I was murdered."

"And you have proof?"

The only victims I'd met so far that had any evidence of being murdered were those of a serial killer, a case I'd worked on and nearly been one of his victims myself. I was kidnapped, but I'd been able to escape only to find myself lost in the woods for days. A search party had formed, so thankfully it wasn't a worse outcome for me.

However, murder was a lofty claim for someone of this gentleman's age, at least without some reason for it. But I had to admit, after Senator Crawford's death, another death I'd helped solve, I shouldn't pass judgment right off the bat.

"I don't need proof." He huffed. "I was in, well, nearly perfect health until a few days ago when I felt ill, and now I'm dead." He tried to slam his hand down on the counter, but it went through it. "Dammit. That's almost as frustrating as being dead."

"I'm so sorry." For a second, I studied him. "I assume you came to me because you think I can help you."

"Yeah, my neighbor and good friend, Daryl, told me you talk to dead people. So here I am."

"Daryl Jackson? His wife is, or was, ReNetta, right?"

"That's the one. He said you could help me."

The Jackson family had been one of my favorite readings. They'd come back a few times. He and his wife had eight children together and a ton of grandchildren plus a few great-grandchildren. It sounded like a wonderful and loving family. With so many people in the family, he always had different people join him.

"Oh, I'm sorry. Did he pass too?" I hoped not.

"No, no. He had talked many times about you after his

readings. About how he got to speak to his wife again and told us all we needed to visit you."

"Nice. I appreciate his referral."

"After we heard about the serial killer and the Redlynne gang case, he said we should all come see you if we pass too, you know, just in case."

My mouth dropped open. While it wasn't the mention of my past cases that caused my surprise, it was the mention of Mr. Jackson suggesting they all come see me if they died. Would a bunch of old dead spirits visit me?

The Redlynne gang had been another murder case I'd worked on. It turned out that they had been the ones to murder my late husband, Ted, and that they were my former in-laws. Crazy case.

I really didn't want to keep solving murders. It was ugly work, but after the closure I felt from solving my late husband's murder, I couldn't deny that to someone else.

Somehow, it actually did fit in with my brand of the medium with a heart. I liked giving closure with love and care to clients, whether through my readings or solving their murders.

Looking at the man's hopeful face had me putting my own feelings aside.

"Yes, yes, I'll help."

"Thank you so much." He sighed. "What a relief. I guess I should properly introduce myself then, since I just barged in here demanding things." He chuckled. "My name is Jack Reynolds."

"It's nice to meet you, Mr. Reynolds."

"No need to call me Mister. Too formal. Call me Jack."

"Okay, Jack." I smiled. "I guess I don't need to introduce myself."

"No, I know you." He smiled, then rubbed his hands together. "So, what's next? Where do we start?"

"First, a few ground rules. This is my home, and while I don't mind you stopping by here, I'd prefer business be done at my office whenever possible. If here, respect rule one: privacy. No popping into my bedroom or bathroom. Deal?"

"Deal."

"So, to start, do you have any ideas about who might have murdered you?" I asked, grabbing a pen and paper so I'd be ready for notes.

"None. Everyone loved me."

Doubtful, but I could only go by his word. I chewed on that for a moment, trying to think of what to ask next.

"As much as I hate to ask, any family?"

"Last of my kind. My wife passed, and we never had children. My siblings are all gone." He beamed, but then he clarified. "They're all dead."

"No enemies or rivals?" Was that the right term? I didn't know.

"Do I seem like the type that has enemies?" He asked. I simply gawked at him, which caused him to frown. "No, no enemies at all."

I tapped the pen on the pad of paper, looking at the blank page. This wouldn't be much of an investigation if he was loved by everyone, and nobody wanted him dead.

Not that I believed his claims. It had been my experience that everyone had at least one person that hated them, even if just a little bit.

"Are you sure you were murdered? This isn't much to look into without some lead." It was nothing, but I didn't want to be a complete pessimist.

"If I knew who did it, I wouldn't be here. I thought you did some magic and then boom, solved."

I gaped at him. Was he serious? It wasn't magic, maybe a bit of luck, my overcurious nature, and my desire to help others. Or like Clint would say, wrong place, wrong time. But it definitely wasn't magic.

"Without some direction, some idea of where to start, I can't do much."

"Well, you can start at Birdsong. That's where the murderer is."

Again, I stared at him. I knew I was going to do this. It would likely mean putting myself in danger and running into Clint, which I couldn't even think about the latter. Neither choice excited me.

"Alright, I'll start there."

"Thank you. I'll get out of your hair now. Let you get to work."

"Alright. Give me a few days to do some research and start digging, then come find me."

He nodded and then disappeared through the side wall. I looked at the spot for a few seconds. How was I going to do this? Why had I agreed?

I guess I'd just start by doing what I always do: hit the internet and see if I could find anything that way, then let my curiosity get me into trouble.

Chapter Two

When we arrived at the crime scene, I stepped out of my partner's car and did a quick scan, taking in the nearly resort-like feel of the location. It was a death at Birdsong Senior Living community.

While the death wasn't suspicious, we always liked to investigate and file the correct paperwork, especially after I nearly lost my job over botched cases.

"Should be standard stuff," Terry said, as he grabbed his keys and a pocket-sized notepad.

"Yeah." I mumbled.

"Still upset?"

"I asked her to marry me, and she said no." I snapped. "Of course I'm still upset."

"Have you tried, oh I don't know, talking to her about it?" Terry asked, brushing off my attitude.

I just stared at him and then opened the door to the main office. I had my ID out before approaching the desk. We knew the drill, but I was not going to answer Terry's asinine question. The last person I wanted to talk to right now was Joanna.

"Hi, Velda. We're here about the death in 1021," Terry said, as he also pulled out his ID.

We knew the staff pretty well since we were here a few times a month. I never enjoyed these calls, but they were a necessary part of our job.

"Hey, boys." She beamed. "Just sign in. So sad about Jack. He was a good one."

She took our IDs and ran them through their scanner to create stick-on badges. It didn't matter that we had our police badges in clear view, they had their procedure, and we had to follow it.

Once they were printed, she passed them to us.

"Do you need me to go with you?" She offered.

"Not necessary. We know our way around." Terry gave a little salute her way as we walked through the back door of the office.

"Thanks for your help." I tried to sound cheerful, but I wasn't feeling it.

We stepped from the office into a spacious courtyard.

Resident apartments were visible from here. We followed one of the covered pathways towards the pool area. Apartment 1021 was in the back, building ten, apartment twenty-one.

Several people greeted us. I couldn't remember most of their names, but they knew us.

"Detectives. It's so good to see you today." One man said. "I guess you're here about Jack."

"That's right. Did you know him?" I asked.

"Yeah, sure did. We played poker together twice a month. He was a cheater but had a good sense of humor."

"The best poker players come off as cheaters," Terry said.

"Did you see him before his death?" I asked, getting back to business.

"Nah, hadn't seen him in a few days. He hadn't been feeling well. Probably caught that bug that's going around."

"Had he seen a doctor?" I asked.

"I don't know. Probably not." He laughed. "We're all old school. No doctors unless you cut something off or our wives make us."

Terry laughed along, but I just stared. Maybe I should have taken a few days off, or at least today. I was in a foul mood.

"Well, thank you." I mumbled as I walked off without a backward look.

As I walked away, I heard Terry apologize for my attitude and offer a better thank you to the man we'd likely never see again until it was time to come sign off on his death.

We took a left near the swimming pool where they had some kind of exercise class going on. A few of the ladies giggled and waved to us. I looked away and focused on the faux cobblestone path that had been stamped on the concrete walkway.

We finally reached the apartment. Well, I did. Terry was stopped by one of the residents. I walked in to find the coroner, Dr. Rodney Starke, already there with a few others I didn't know. Perhaps they were with Dr. Rodney.

"Hey, Doc." I said, offering him my hand. He held up his gloved hands. "Oh, sorry, of course."

"So, where's Walden?"

"He got stopped by one of the ladies. They love him here."

"Ah, yes, the lonely widows." He chuckled. "Well, I've already pronounced him, and we took pictures. As usual, I'll make sure y'all get copies."

"Thanks." I looked over his shoulder towards the bedroom. "Died in his sleep?"

"Looks that way. Nothing suspicious from what I can tell."

"Next of kin?"

"None to speak of, but Kelli here was a close friend." He nodded towards a woman standing in the kitchen crying. "Good luck." He chuckled and went to speak to a young woman with a camera.

Must be the new assistant he'd told me about last time. She was young, but everyone in their early twenties looked like babies to me now, and I was only thirty-three.

My mom always told me I was an old soul, always seemed older than my biological age, which would explain how I made detective so young. The youngest in Creekview.

I didn't usually think about it, but seeing the recent college graduate laughing with her boss, I suddenly felt ancient.

I turned back to look at Kelli. She looked to be closer to my age, maybe even a bit older. She had dark hair cut into a short, spiky style. Her clothing was probably called boho style, but I only knew that because of Joanna.

She loved fashion and had stacks of magazines around. Though she mostly wore casual clothes herself, she still loved to look at all the various styles.

I chastised myself for thinking of Jo again. Since Terry still hadn't joined me, I shook off the thoughts of what could have been and instead took the few steps over to speak to Kelli.

When I got close to her, I could tell that she was indeed older than me. I would peg her at around forty-five. She tried to give the appearance of youth with her hairstyle and clothing.

"Hi, Kelli, right?"

"Yes, that's right." She flashed a weak smile. "Kelli with an I."

"I see. So, Kelli with an I..."

She giggled before I could continue. "You're funny."

"Um, thanks. So, Dr. Rodney said you were good friends with the deceased?"

Tears formed in her eyes. "I was. He was like a father to me."

"Oh, I'm sorry." I tried to look sympathetic, but all I wanted was to get this day over with and start out fresh tomorrow. "And how did you know him?"

"I work here. I'm the Event and Activities Director."

"I didn't know. I've never met you before. Have you been here long?"

"Yeah, a few years now, but I guess I haven't been involved in one of these before."

I just nodded. "So, he had no next of kin from what Doc says. Do you know of any family?"

"No, none. His wife died a few years ago, and they never had children. His parents are long gone, and he had a brother who passed, um, maybe ten years ago? He had children, but unfortunately, they're gone as well. If there is anyone else, he never said, and I never met them."

I looked around, trying to think of what else to ask. "We bumped into a gentleman on the way here. He mentioned that Mr. Reynolds had been sick for the last few days. Do you know anything about that?"

"Oh, yes, he was complaining of an upset stomach, headache, and fatigue. It didn't seem too serious. He still came to watercolors class two days ago. Then I saw him yesterday when I dropped off some soup for him." She dabbed at her eyes as a few tears slipped. "I just can't believe he's gone. He was one of my favorites here."

Thankfully, Terry joined us at that moment. He was so much better with crying women than I was, and honestly better at a lot of this communication stuff in general.

"This is my partner, Detective Terry Walden. Terry with a Y," I quipped. Terry gave me a sideways look, but I ignored him.

"Oh, Detective, you're so funny." She grabbed my bicep and squeezed it. "Hi, partner Terry."

"Nice to meet you. Clint, we need to meet with Dr. Rodney before he leaves," he said.

"We'll be in touch if we have any further questions." I said to Kelli before joining Doc and his team in the bedroom.

A few hours later, the body had been taken by the coroner's office and would be handled there. We had gathered limited evidence, mostly just facts, and would wait for Dr. Rodney's autopsy results. On the surface, it looked like natural causes.

Once we had made our way safely out of Birdsong, and after receiving only a few marriage proposals from the ladies there, Terry turned to me as he pulled onto the main road.

"What was that with that woman?"

"Which one?" We'd bumped into a dozen in our time there.

"The one in the apartment. Terry with a Y, what was that about?"

"Oh, nothing. She introduced herself as Kelli with an I, so I just kept with it."

"So much for being broken-hearted over Joanna," he chastised me.

"I am!" I growled.

He chuckled. "Couldn't tell with all that sexual tension between you two."

"Not even. I was just trying to lighten the mood. She kept crying."

"Well, you sure lightened it alright. I think she was already naming your imaginary children."

"Oh, boy. I didn't mean... I was just trying to... You know what? It doesn't matter. I'm never getting serious with a woman again. I'm done. Plus, she's at least ten years older than me." I crossed my arms over my chest and stared out the window, letting my vision blur.

"Yeah, maybe, but I've heard that before. The part about not getting serious."

That was it. We didn't talk about it again.

Chapter Three

~ Joanna ~

It had been a few days since Jack Reynolds came to see me. I hadn't yet done any research on him, but I decided before Oakley woke and I got on with my day, I would start looking into his death.

If I was going to take on his murder investigation, I wanted to know more about him. Plus, I hoped there would be more information about his death out now that he'd been gone a few days.

Thankfully, I already knew a bit about Birdsong, having explored it as an option for my parents. That meant I could focus this short search session solely on Jack.

I pulled out my laptop to see if I could learn about him.

"Alright, Mr. Jack Reynolds, let's see what you're all about."

I typed his name in the search box and several articles popped up. The first few were about his death from just days ago. The initial reports were saying heart attack but waiting on autopsy. Nothing special. Nothing that said murder.

I sighed.

It was the next articles that caught my eye, though. He'd been the CEO of an extremely successful technology company, ReynHarp Software and Technology, that he'd founded with a partner in 1980. He'd retired a few years ago and had remained on the board.

"No children and his wife passed a few years ago..." I read on. His wealth was left to his good friend, Kelli Wallace, Event and Activities Director at Birdsong. "Well, that's interesting. He just passed away two days ago and they're already reporting about this."

I made a mental note, then continued reading a few more articles about him and his life. Nothing else really stood out to me, but he seemed to have had an interesting life of traveling with his wife and friends, famous connections, and a successful business.

My searching was cut short when Oakley announced that she was awake.

"Ma! Ma!" came her sweet voice over the monitor, so I closed my browser and went to her room to get her ready for our outing.

"Hey, baby girl," I said when I walked in the room. "Are you ready to get up?"

"Uppp, up."

I got her changed and tamed her bed head, then carried her to the kitchen for her breakfast.

I handed her a bottle and added her favorite cereal to the tray of her highchair. Then I cut up a banana, which was always a favorite, and she'd be covered in the sweet mush before it was all eaten.

She drank a bit before grabbing a few pieces of cereal and then reached for the banana. Chewy assumed his position under her chair, waiting for the handouts that were sure to come his way.

This was my favorite time of the day. The part before we really got moving, and it was just the three of us.

I watched them a few more moments, before grabbing my laptop again. I did a bit more digging, but there was nothing new about him. Even his obituary didn't offer much.

"Ugh, this seems like a dead end."

"Well, that's ironic, isn't it? Since I am dead." Jack's voice startled me.

"Jack, what are you doing here?"

"You said come see you in a few days. It's been a few days."

"I meant at my office. Not my house."

"You didn't say that, and I don't even know where your office is."

I rolled my eyes. "Well, you're here now, so what's going on?"

"You tell me."

"Tell you what?"

"Who murdered me?"

"It's only been a few days. How would I know? Heck, the police probably haven't even started looking at it as murder. They'll probably wait for the autopsy."

"Why would you say that? I was murdered."

"They likely don't have probable cause to think that. You said it yourself; you have no enemies, so there are likely no clues to point towards murder."

I knew enough about their murder investigations at this point to know that.

"Then they aren't very good at their job." He huffed.

I just stared at him. From what I'd read about him, I got the impression he was a go-getter and was used to getting his way.

"What can you tell me about this Kelli Wallace at Birdsong? You left her your estate?"

"Oh, yes, Kelli. She was like the daughter I never had." He smiled while putting his hand over his heart. "I'd initially planned to leave it to my business partner, Rueben, but he was recently diagnosed with lung cancer, so I had it changed about six or seven months ago to Kelli. She's such a dear."

"Did she know that you'd left the money to her? I mean before you died, did she know?"

"No, I wanted it to be a surprise. I just didn't know I would die so quickly. I thought I would live to be a hundred."

"Well, eighty-five is pretty darn good."

"Maybe."

"Do you think Kelli would have killed you for the money?"

"No, of course not! Why would you even say that?"

"I don't know. It always seems to be someone close to the victim, and in my limited experience, money is the source of a lot of evil."

"Yeah, well, you don't know Kelli. She's not like that."

"Okay, well, you need to give me something to work with here. Without at least one suspect, what am I supposed to think?"

"It's probably one of those crazy women at Birdsong. They all thought they were in love with me."

Love was the other thing that seemed to make people crazy and kill, so maybe that was it. Laney had said they were all drama queens.

"Names?"

"All of them."

"Look, I'm sure you were a great guy, but all the women at Birdsong couldn't have been that crazy in love with you."

"I was a playboy. I was smart, had money, good-looking. I had two good hips still, too."

"Okay, even if they were all in love with you, can you give me a few names?"

"Odette. Diana, Robin, maybe Dawn? Claudette. Suzanne. Alma Jean. Marie. Um, Edith. Mary Louise. Thelma."

I put my hand up. He stopped. I tried not to mention or notice that one of those named ladies was Laney's grandmother. I would deal with that later.

"So, are you just going to name all the ladies?"

"This is your job. You go there and talk to them. Then you'll know."

This guy was arrogant, and like a few of the spirits I'd already worked with, I didn't think I liked him much. But if there was a murderer at Birdsong, I would have to look for another senior community for my parents.

This one was the best in the area, though. None of the others even came close to the amenities offered at Birdsong.

"Okay, okay. I'm going for a tour there soon, so I'll ask around then."

"Great, then I'll be back in a few days." He turned to leave. "Wait, where's your office?"

I gave him the address, then he said goodbye, leaving through the wall. I stared at it for a moment, then turned towards my daughter.

She'd finished her breakfast and was sipping the last of her bottle. We were in the transition to sippy cups, but I still gave her one at breakfast.

She was used to me talking to myself, though it was really spirits. Someday I might have to explain it to her, but thankfully for now, she was still too young.

I got her cleaned up and ready for the day. Janie, her nanny, would be here soon, and then I'd be off to work.

My cell phone chimed. It was my sister, Audrey.

Lunch today?

Yes, please

I hadn't seen my sister in a week or so. She hadn't gotten the full Clint proposal story and likely wanted the scoop.

I didn't know if I was ready to relive it again, but she was one of my best friends and my sister, so I knew I'd tell her, and she would give me honest feedback on it.

On one hand, I felt so stupid for my decision. I didn't really want to end our relationship, but just wanted him to give me a reason to say yes.

His reason was because he thought that's what I wanted and because Oakley had been calling him Dada. Granted, I should have stopped that, but I figured she was too young right now to fully understand it.

Was it too much to expect to have just one conversation about our future together? Given that we both had some drama in our past relationships, it only made sense to me.

"Knock, knock." Janie said as she opened the front door.

Chewy rushed to her and laid at her feet for belly rubs. Oakley squealed and toddled over.

"Up!"

"Good morning, Janie."

"Good morning, Jo."

"She's had breakfast and is ready for the day."

"Great. We're going to have fun." She bounced Oakley, causing her to giggle.

"I know you will." I kissed the baby's head and then headed to the office.

As I drove, I thought about my conversation with Jack. I needed to get over to Birdsong and soon if I was going to find clues about his death. I was sure I wouldn't be able to get into his apartment, so I was going to have to depend on speaking to people.

It made sense what he said about this Kelli person. I guessed without other family members, leaving it to someone he loved and trusted was the right thing to do. I just hoped he would come back with fewer names, not just everyone.

I got to work and immediately jumped into answering emails, approving checks and vendor orders, and of course, client readings.

At lunchtime, I had an hour's break, so Audrey agreed to bring me lunch and we would eat in the breakroom.

"I brought enough for Micah and Tessa if they want to join us."

"I brought lunch, but I'll eat with y'all," Tessa said.

"Thanks, but I have to pass. I'm going to meet Josh for a quick lunch. We have a few wedding details to go over," Micah said.

"Oh, that's exciting. I can't wait to hear all about it." I smiled.

He left and the three of us got settled at the breakroom tables.

"So, has she told you much about what happened with Clint?" Audrey asked Tessa as if I wasn't here.

"Not much. Just that he asked, and she said no."

They both turned toward me.

"What?" I flashed a grin.

"Don't give me 'what,' sis. Spill it."

Tessa drummed her fingers on the table.

"Okay, fine. Just so you know, this isn't gossip to me. It really broke my heart."

"I know." Audrey reached for my hand, giving it a squeeze. "So, tell us what happened so we can talk you through it."

"Fine."

I told them the story much as I had Laney. They didn't interrupt much, letting me get it all out plus a few tears along the way.

"Wow, I'm so sorry. I think you did the right thing, though," Audrey said.

"I agree. I mean, you had mostly kept things casual from what I could tell," Tessa added.

"And that's basically what I'd said to him. We never once talked about marriage or even living together. Nothing about taking things more seriously."

"Well, he did stay with you after you were shot that one time."

"True, but it was only to help me out with the baby. She was still so little then."

"I would have stayed with you," Tessa said.

"You could have also stayed with us," Audrey offered.

"Maybe, but that's in the past, and staying with me a few weeks wasn't living together. Plus, he slept in the other room."

Audrey and Tessa smirked at each other.

"Okay, so now what? Y'all are just broken up?" Audrey asked. "That doesn't seem right."

I shrugged. I had nothing else I could say until Clint and I got a chance to talk again. But who knew when that would be?

Of course, depending on Jack's death, it could be sooner than I thought.

"Well, I'm having a hard time believing that's it for you two," Audrey said. "I'm cheering for y'all to get back together."

"Um." I didn't really answer.

We wrapped up lunch. It was nice to spend time with my sister and friend. They hadn't given me any groundbreaking advice about Clint, but I didn't feel so lonely in my heartbreak.

Chapter Four

Friday was my day off. I would be meeting Laney at Birdsong for lunch with her grandmother and a tour of the facility.

"Do you want to bring your parents too?" Laney asked when she called to let me know she'd arranged the tour.

"I'm still trying to get them to even consider it, so I'm thinking if I have a look around first, then I could sell them on it better."

"Sounds good. See you there tomorrow."

The truth was I wanted a look around to learn more about Jack's life. My parents would have been a distraction.

I pulled up to Birdsong a few minutes early. It was like pulling up to a resort hotel. Perfectly manicured landscaping, all the flowers in bloom. There was a sparkling blue fountain in the middle of a circular driveway that led in various directions.

"Wow. It's gorgeous."

I took the fork towards the visitor parking lot as Laney instructed, found an empty spot, then sent her a text as I didn't see her car nearby.

Almost immediately after hitting send, my phone rang.

"Hey, Laney. I'm here."

"Great. Go into the office and I'll meet you there in a second or two."

"Okay, I'll see you there."

We hung up, and I grabbed my purse.

The property seemed expansive, but I only had a limited view from the parking lot. The buildings I could see were a blueish gray stucco with bright white trim and terracotta tiled roofs.

From here, I could also see some of the resident balconies. They looked like typical apartment complexes with various decor dotting them, such as patio furniture, potted plants, and a few had grills. No two were exactly alike. You could definitely see the different personalities.

"Hello, welcome to Birdsong." A cheerful woman behind the reception desk greeted me. "How may I help you?"

"She's with me, Velda," Laney said as she stepped through a door at the far side of the lobby area.

"Oh, Mrs. Landon, hello. Nice to see you." Velda smiled at her and then turned back to me. "I'll just need your driver's license to get you signed in."

I fumbled in my hot mess of a purse for the license, then handed it to her with a smile. She typed into their computer. I heard a printer start up. She went to a small label printer behind her and pulled off a sticker badge for me.

"Here you go, Ms. Webber," she said, handing me the sticker and my license back. "Enjoy your visit."

I placed the sticker on my shirt and followed Laney through the door she'd only just come through. It led to a beautifully landscaped courtyard. More resident apartments were visible here. These had a nice view of one of the swimming pools and a lush garden.

I could see residents moving around doing their daily things. There were also a number of spirits following them. I tried not to make eye contact with the ghosts. It would just start up a conversation that I didn't want to have at the moment.

"Hi, Mrs. Turner," Laney greeted a resident as we started to walk from the office.

"Hiya, Laney. Where is that beautiful daughter of yours today?" the older lady asked.

"She's with the sitter. I brought my friend to have a look around. This is Joanna Webber," she said, gesturing to me.

"Oh, Joanna, the medium with a heart. I've seen your show before."

"Oh, well, it's nice to meet you." I said with my best Joanna, medium with a heart smile.

She looked around and then whispered, "Is my husband here with us?"

"Um," I looked at the man standing nearby. He nodded. "Yes, he's right here." I gestured behind her.

She jumped as she looked to the spot I gestured to. "Alan?"

"Yes, I'm here, Margo," I spoke for him.

"Oh, Alan, I'm so glad you're here. I have missed you."

"I've been with you since I passed. I will be by your side until the day you join me on this side."

Tears formed in her eyes. "I love you, Alan, my love. I miss you so much. The kids and especially our grandchildren miss you too."

"I love and miss you all too, Margo," I said for Alan.

Margo produced a tissue seemingly out of thin air and dabbed her eyes.

"Oh, Joanna, thank you for being here today. I needed to have a small piece of him today." She smiled and looked over to where Alan stood, then back to me. "Can I hug you?"

"Yes, of course." We hugged. She smelled of powder and a rose scented perfume. It was comforting. I smiled as the embrace ended. "You're welcome. I'm glad to give you some words of love."

Laney and I continued to walk through the courtyard.

"I'm still not used to that," she teased.

"What? The spontaneous reading?"

She nodded. "Yeah, I mean I know you can do that and I'm a true believer, but it's still startling at times."

"Honestly, it is for me too."

There were seniors doing yoga in a grassy space to our left. A few looked our way, but most were too focused to notice. We walked a short way from there and I noticed a small group playing cards and smoking.

A few were using those e-cigarettes or maybe vape pens? I didn't know much about them, but it caught my attention as there was a fruity smell when we walked by.

We then passed a large room that looked like an art studio. I stopped to peek in the window.

"That's the craft room. They always have something going on," Laney said.

"Looks fun."

It looked like there was a group making spring wreaths. One lady with dark, spiky hair waved to us and then jogged over to the door.

"Hey, Ms. Laney. Good to see you today. Here for a visit with your gramma?"

"Hi, yes, and I brought my friend with me today."

"Oh, I know you. Joanna, the medium with a heart." The woman smiled brightly and then leaned forward to hug me without asking. "Nice to have you here today. I'm Kelli. I'm the Events and Activities Director."

"Nice to meet you." I smiled.

It was on the tip of my tongue to ask her about Jack Reynolds, but I kept it to myself for now. If the conversation came around to an appropriate time to bring it up, then I might.

"Do you want to look around?" She offered.

"Sure," I said, but I looked at Laney for confirmation.

She nodded, so we stepped inside. The scent of floral perfumes mixed with the smell of strong glue, paint, and wood they were crafting with hit like a brick wall. I tried not to gag on the strong odor.

"We're making birdhouses that will go out in the courtyards."

"Oh, they're nice. I love this idea," I said.

"I always like to come up with fun things to make or do. We do a lot of seasonal and holiday crafts."

I smiled at a few of the residents who had stopped what they were doing to watch us. They didn't smile back, just looked at Kelli. I guessed they didn't appreciate the intrusion on their craft time.

"Hey, everyone. I'd like to introduce Joanna and Laney. Y'all know Alma Jean, right?" Kelli said. "Well, Laney is her granddaughter."

"And you're that Medium!" one of the ladies blurted out.

"She is!" another shouted.

The room erupted into chaos as they all started crowding around me and shouting out requests. I tried to back away because between the smell, the sudden movement, and all the voices shouting at me, both alive and dead, it was overwhelming.

"Calm down, everyone. Give her some room," Kelli yelled above the senior citizen mosh pit.

It took a moment, but once the seniors had settled, Kelli spoke up. "Maybe I can meet with Joanna and discuss getting her to come do a group reading here. Not just an ambush style one. How does that sound?"

She looked at the residents, and then everyone turned to me.

"I would be happy to come back out and do a group reading for as many people as I can." I smiled. "Do you have a card? I can have my assistant call you to set it up."

"Yes. Next door in my office," she nodded.

We followed her out of the craft room and into the fresh air. I took in a deep breath to calm my stomach and head. Smells always got to me, but more so when combined with the crushing crowd of people, both alive and dead. It was sensory overload.

We stepped into her office. It was packed with boxes and bags overflowing with various crafting supplies. On the walls were watercolor paintings, small wreaths, and needlepoints as well as many other fun, homemade artwork.

"Here you go. Just have her call me. I'm here most days until about five or six."

"Thanks. I will." I took the card and slipped it into my purse. "I always love doing the group readings."

"I lost someone recently too, and I'd love to hear from him." Her eyes became watery as she spoke.

"Jack Reynolds?" I asked.

"Yes, how'd you... Is he here?" She looked around.

"Oh, no, sorry. I heard on the news and just thought I saw you were friends with him."

"Oh, right." She grabbed a tissue from a floral box on her desk. "We had become friends while he lived here. He loved watercolors."

She looked over at one picture on her wall. I followed her gaze to see a sunset with the name Jack written at the bottom.

"It's beautiful."

"Thanks. He didn't have any family left, so he sort of adopted me as a daughter. A lot of the residents are lonely and looking for someone to fill that void. That's why I love my job. I can give them a fun day and create memories with them."

I understood a little of how she felt. That was what I hoped to do for people, but in a slightly different way by giving them closure in their grief and passing on messages of love and peace.

"That sounds wonderful, and I'm sure they love and appreciate what you do."

"I like to think so." She smiled. "I count some of them, like Jack, as my close friends. Almost like family."

"Laney, oh Laney!" We heard someone call from behind us.

"Oh, Grandma, sorry. We stopped to talk to Kelli," Laney said.

"I thought you got lost."

"No, Joanna hasn't been here before, so I was just giving her a quick tour on the way, and as I said, we stopped to say hello to Kelli,"

Laney said.

"Yes, I'm sorry, Alma Jean. It was my fault for getting them sidetracked." She smiled. "I've asked Joanna if she would like to come back and do a group reading for us sometime."

"That would be wonderful. I would love to hear from my Harold," Alma Jean said, looking at me.

I looked around, but no Harold stepped forward. I simply shook my head.

"Well, I'll let y'all get on to lunch. I need to get back to my class, anyway." Kelli waved and turned back towards the classroom.

"Shall we?" Alma Jean nodded, hooked her arms with both of us. Laney on one side and me on her other. That was Alma Jean, always loving and fun, wanting to include everyone.

She chatted as we walked to her apartment.

"So, I thought we'd lunch in the bistro today. I already set us up a reservation with them because it tends to get packed on Fridays. We have a lot of visitors today." She giggled, squeezing her arms a little. "We call it family day around here."

"I would think the weekends would be busy too, no?" I asked.

"Sometimes, but many of the families have children in activities like baseball, football, or scouts, so families are busy with their young ones. We have a number of residents who drive, so they may go to the games or activities on the weekend. Then we have others who get picked up on Friday and then dropped back off on Sunday. Not everyone does that, but enough that it actually gets almost quiet here on the weekends."

I simply nodded. We reached her apartment. The outside was decorated for Valentine's Day, which had been a few days ago.

Alma Jean caught my stare. "I will be switching this out soon with spring decor. We have contests for who has the best seasonal displays."

"Oh, that's fun." My mother would love that. She had a huge collection of decorations for all the seasons.

Looking around at the other residents here, my parents would be on the younger side, but I still felt this was the right move for them, especially given all the fun things they did here. That would keep them busy.

Alma Jean pushed open her door.

"You don't lock your door?" I asked.

"No, dear, I have nothing anyone wants, but honestly nobody around here locks them. Only when we're gone for more than a few hours." She laughed. "Well, come in, make yourself at home."

"Can I show Jo around? She's trying to talk her parents into moving here."

"Certainly. Just don't go snooping in my drawers unless you want to know far too much about your grandmother." She winked at Laney.

"Ew, Gramma!" Laney giggled.

Alma Jean lived in a one-bedroom, one-bathroom unit with a small porch off the back. The porch area had a small metal garden table with two chairs and loads of plants. She clearly had a green thumb. I could barely keep my one pothos alive.

The unit was a nice size for one person. I noticed all the kitchen appliances were full-sized, not the smaller apartment versions. There was ample counter and cabinet space. My mom would love this. I'd expected it all to be smaller.

"Are most of the kitchens about this size?" I looked over at Alma Jean.

"More or less. Some of the three-bedrooms have larger ones, but there aren't many of those units. Most are one- and two-bedrooms," she said from her seat in a floral club chair.

"Makes sense."

We visited in her apartment for a bit longer before heading to the bistro for lunch. At lunch, we met a few of Alma Jean's friends, Odette and Robin.

It was hard to follow the conversation amongst the three best friends. They jumped quickly from topic to topic, often starting in the middle as if it was a discussion started hours earlier that they were just getting around to finishing.

I wasn't sure how they got on the topic of Jack, but I was thankful for it. Perhaps it would give me something to go on. The one thing I learned was that Odette had been in a relationship with him, at least until it soured.

"It all started when that new hussy moved into 1143," Odette hissed. "She thinks she is so hot because she's new here, has two good hips, and can still drive."

Jack had mentioned he had good hips. I guessed that was important at this age.

"Oh yeah, she's making the rounds," Alma Jean added with a click of her tongue.

"She has all the men eating out of her hand," Robin added.

"She vapes like the kids do," Odette said, raising an eyebrow.

"So do you, Odette," Robin smirked.

"Not like she does. I just use it to help me quit smoking. She uses all those flavors."

"You've been quitting since I've known you," Robin teased.

"Oh, hush." Odette chuckled, smacking Robin's arm lightly.

"Did I tell you I got the lab work back from my appointment the other day?" Alma Jean said.

I didn't know who the hussy in 1143 was, but clearly she wasn't popular with the ladies. With the shift in conversation, I didn't get a chance to ask more about her or Jack. Though she seemed like a minor annoyance to the three friends as they hadn't spent much time discussing her.

Overall, it was a nice day, and though I didn't learn much about Jack, at least I got my questions answered for my parents and booked a job that would give me another opportunity to come visit. Maybe then I could learn something.

Chapter Five

"Knock, knock." The Chief said at my office door. "Got a minute?"

"Hey, Chief." I stood. "Do you want to sit here or meet in your office?"

He looked around my tiny closet of an office. "Let's go to mine, if you don't mind."

I nodded and followed him. I didn't blame him at all. His office was three times the size and had actual air flowing through it. Mine felt like a stale phone booth with furniture in it, but it was way better than the open concept bullpen. No privacy, and you had to stare into the face of a dozen others while trying to work, which was not productive. I was thankful for my airless box most of the time.

"Have a seat, Hartley." Chief said as he walked around to his large leather chair. "Alright, so what's up with you and the Medium?"

"Um, what do you mean?"

I didn't know what he'd heard, and I'd been careful not to speak to anyone other than Terry. I'd also tried to keep my mood in check so as not to bring personal issues to work, though I'd had my grumpy moments, just like anyone else.

"A few weeks ago, you were dating, then Walden asks me about making her a consultant, which I was highly considering, but now I hear you're no longer together. What's the deal?"

"Ah, well, we broke up."

"Mutually?"

I wasn't sure why that mattered, but I held back that question. Instead, I said, "I guess you could say that."

"But would you say that?" He pointed his meaty finger my way. "What I'm asking is if I hired her to consult on some of the homicide cases, would you have a problem working with her?"

I sat back hard in the chair. Was our split mutual?

When I proposed, her expression said more than the words. It was crushing.

She asked why I thought we were ready for marriage, which caught me off guard and I ended up giving some lame answer. When she suggested we take a break, I merely walked away. Did that make it mutual?

The bigger question of whether I could work with her was harder to answer and easier at the same time. I was a professional, so I could work with anyone, even if begrudgingly, but if she was put in a dangerous situation again, I would lose my mind.

Then again, if I was working more closely with her, I could keep her out of trouble, right?

I knew the answer to that was no. When Joanna put her mind on something, not much was going to stand in her way, and her natural curiosity would always lead her down the wrong path.

"Yes, I can work with her."

"Wonderful!" He boomed. "I'd like you to go speak to her about it. Here is the offer and contract if she says yes."

He passed me an envelope. With my hands shaking, I took it.

"I'll speak to her soon."

"The sooner the better. We don't want to miss any more suspects, like that Hammersley woman. Had we caught her sooner, she'd be in prison right now instead of rotting down at the cemetery."

I nodded, stood, and walked slowly back to my office. I dropped heavily into my chair and let my hands fall into my lap with the letter falling loose to the floor.

"Rough day?" Walden said, coming in and picking up the paper as he did. He placed it on the desk.

"You could say that."

"I guess Chief just talked to you."

"Yeah, and he wants me to go speak to her about it." I sighed. "I haven't seen her since..."

"Do you want me to join you?"

"No, I really need to be the one. We have other things to talk about anyway, and plus I have a birthday gift for Oakley." A pain stabbed my heart as I looked up at him. "I can't believe she's nearly a year old."

"It goes so fast." And he would know with four of his own.

"I've always heard that but didn't understand."

I looked to the small, framed picture of me holding her just a month ago. We were looking at each other, and a second after Jo took the picture, Oakley laid a big, slobbery baby kiss on my cheek.

"When are you going to talk to her?"

"I honestly don't know."

Next weekend would be her birthday party, and would have been a chance to see her, but while I'd initially been invited, now I wasn't sure I would attend. I couldn't look at Jo or Oakley without pain.

Knowing Joanna, she would be busy all week with preparations for the party. She and Laney were doing a joint celebration for both girls.

However, Chief would want me to talk to her before then anyway, so I'd have to get over myself and just call her.

"My offer still stands if you want me to go with you, just say the word."

"Thanks."

My desk phone buzzed. "Hartley."

"Need you and Walden on the East side. Homicide. Two victims."

I wrote down the address that dispatch provided. Terry ran over to his office while I finished up with dispatch. When I was done on the phone, I grabbed my gear and met Terry in the hallway.

"Ready?" He said, keys in hand.

"Yep."

We headed over to the East side of town to an apartment complex. The patrol officers had the scene secured and media were setting up beyond the barrier the team established.

We parked and went to find the lead officer.

"Looks like a home invasion. Total of three victims, but two deceased. One is en route to the hospital. We're speaking to witnesses now." Officer Williams said, gesturing towards her partner, Officer Bishop. "We have officers canvassing the area." She gave us the vague description of the suspects.

Two males, medium build. One slightly taller than the other. Both in dark clothes with their faces covered.

"Thanks, Williams." Terry said. "What about security cameras?"

"Apartment manager is downloading it for us now. Wright is with him."

I left them there so I could start talking to the other officers and check out the scene. We would gather our data and Terry would speak to the media. Fairly standard stuff, but with a suspect on the run, we'd need to solve this quickly.

Once the security footage was downloaded, we had our technology team get screenshots of the suspects and start circulating with the news outlets.

With the officers out searching the area, we should catch them, I hoped. I sometimes missed that adrenaline rush of being a patrol officer, of searching for suspects, but I'd have to stay put until I was done with the crime scene.

Hours later, they arrested the two suspects. The arresting officers would report on them while Terry and I reported the facts of the deaths. Nothing surprising or out of the ordinary for this type of thing, but it kept my mind off of Joanna for several hours.

It wasn't until I got home that night and saw the gift bag with a puppy wearing a birthday hat on it and the pink and blue tissue paper shoved in it, that I let my mind go to two of my favorite people.

"Should I text her?" I said to the happy bag puppy.

Of course, it didn't reply, but if it could, it would probably tell me no. Though I knew I would have to see her sometime soon, I wouldn't disturb their party.

I'd text her later to see when I could stop by, or when we could meet up. Maybe somewhere public so it didn't get too personal.

The Chief would want me to have this conversation with her soon, but I just didn't know if I was ready. It took me years to get over Monica, and not until Joanna. I hadn't felt that connection with any of the women I'd met between the two, so she wasn't someone I expected would be easy to get over.

I sighed and headed for a beer, then kicked my shoes off before heading to my bedroom to change out of my work clothes. Now in shorts and a t-shirt, I headed back to my living room, turning on the television and flipping through the program guide until I found a historical documentary about World War II. Something tactical and strategic to focus on versus the pain in my heart.

I stood there watching and drinking my beer a moment before pulling out my phone to order some dinner. Cooking for one wasn't always fun. Wings, a good war documentary, and cold beer sounded like a good way to end the work week and my long day.

Chapter Six

The weekend had flown by in a flash of party planning. It still felt like we had so much to do. On Friday, I would help Laney get her house ready, but really there wasn't much else I could do this week until then.

I sighed and headed into the office to start my Monday.

"Good morning, Tessa." I said when I came inside. I looked to the security desk, expecting to see Percy, our usual guard. "Oh, hey, Eddie. Where's Percy today?"

"He had an appointment, so I'm all yours." He grinned.

He had a bright, friendly smile with perfect white teeth and one dimple on his left cheek. I blushed and looked away.

"Oh, thank you." I smiled and hurried to Tessa's desk. "Schedule in my chair?" I said to Tessa.

"Sorry. Nope." She held up a piece of paper. "Right here. I didn't make it back there yet."

"Perfect. Thank you." I took it and headed to my office. I felt my face warm as I was sure Eddie was watching me walk away.

Until he'd asked me out for coffee a few weeks ago, I would have never thought of him in any other way but goofy Eddie. Since then, I'd been noticing how cute he was and the way he looked at me when I was in the room. His eyes would twinkle, and his smile would brighten. Had he always looked at me that way?

"Alright, boss, who made you blush like that?" Micah's voice teased.

"Oh, gosh." I put my hands on my face. "Nobody. Just warm from outside."

"Likely story. It's winter." He tapped his foot. "Is it Eddie?"

My face got hotter. I was sure it was three times brighter too. "Um."

"It is. He is cute. If you like that dad bod type, which I know for a fact you do."

"Okay, fine." I pushed him playfully but firmly into his office and followed behind. I whispered. "He asked me out a few weeks ago, but I said no since I was still dating Clint. I'd never thought of him as more than a friend."

"So, what changed?"

"I started thinking of him as more than a friend. Obviously."

"Obviously." He giggled.

"It's just a little crush though. I mean, I still have feelings for Clint. This is just a silly thing that will pass."

He smirked. "I believe you."

"Did you get that order placed?" I said, trying to change the subject.

"Smooth, boss, but yes, I did. Order should arrive next Thursday."

"Perfect."

I left his office, heading first for some coffee and then went to my office to start the day. A few hours later and two readings complete, Tessa came in my office.

"Hey, Jo. I just got off the phone with Kelli from Birdsong. We're scheduled to do a group reading there at 2 pm next Friday. Good?"

"Great. On my calendar?" I lived by my calendar.

"Of course." She smiled.

"You're the best."

After she left, I went to the reading room to get it set up for the next appointment who should be here any minute. I put out fresh bottles of water and a few snacks because I knew this client had young children with them.

"Plenty of tissues. Pillows fluffed. Perfect." I was about to step out of the room when movement caught my eye. "Jack?"

"Finally, I've caught up with you."

"Hi, yes, it's been a while."

"You're a tough lady to keep up with." He grumbled. "So, have you figured out who killed me yet?"

Straight to the point. The little I'd learned about him, this didn't surprise me. He was a shrewd businessman.

"No, it's only been about a week or so. As I said last time, it doesn't work that fast. Plus, you didn't give me much to go on."

"I thought you were smart. I'm so disappointed."

"Hey, I am smart. That has nothing to do with this." I wanted to stomp my foot, but it felt childish. "Usually there's a list of suspects, or at least one. You told me everyone loves you, and the list you did give me was starting to be everyone. That isn't much to go on. In fact, it's nothing."

"Did you go to Birdsong and talk to anyone there?"

"Yes, I met Kelli and Alma Jean, Robin, Odette, and a few others."

"Isn't Kelli the best?" I nodded but didn't reply. He continued. "But those others didn't like me. Odette was obsessed with me. Couldn't get enough, but I had no interest. I still love my wife even though she's been gone for more than six years."

The way he said it was so sweet and heartwarming that I found myself placing my hand over my heart.

"That's very sweet. Have you found her in the afterlife to reconnect?"

"No, I haven't, and frankly, until I figure this out, I don't want to."

Before I could ask him why, Tessa stuck her head into the hallway from reception. She whispered, "Client is here."

"I'm coming." I whispered back. "Jack, I don't have time now, but you can stick around or come back after 3. I'll have more time, and really, please, think of who might want you dead."

Maybe that was harsh, but how could he not have someone? I could name at least three people right now who would be on my list. One of them was Vera Beckett, who was the most recent person to kidnap me and hold me at gunpoint. Even though she was in jail at the moment, I knew she hated me for my part in getting her locked up.

Her mother, Irene, was trying to get her an insanity deal, but honestly, she needed more than just that. The poor girl needed a lot of therapy and a break from social media. At least one of those she was getting from behind bars.

I left Jack standing there so I could go greet my guests and do the reading for them. I needed to be focused so I could hear the messages and pass them on accurately.

"Hi, King family." I said, stepping into the lobby, careful not to look over at Eddie.

The family smiled, stood, and joined me at the door.

"Thank you so much, Ms. Joanna." The mother of the group said. "I have been missing my husband so very much."

As we walked to the reading room, she introduced me to her

children, grandchildren, and even one tiny great-grandchild.

"You have a beautiful family." I smiled as I gestured for them to have a seat.

Her husband, Leroy, joined us but seemed perturbed that Jack had stayed in the room with us.

"This is my time, sir. You gotta move along," Leroy said.

"I'm just waiting my turn with the medium. I won't say a peep, and only you, me, and her will know if you would just pipe down," Jack nearly growled.

"Who are you telling to pipe down?" Leroy snapped back.

The two ghosts started to bicker. I smiled nervously at the family. "Sorry, I'm having a slight problem connecting. Give me just a moment."

I took a deep breath in, then slowly exhaled. Stalling the best I could until the two men came to an agreement. Jack could stay, but if he said a word, he had to leave.

His attitude gave me a good idea of the type of person Jack had been, and so perhaps not everyone had loved him as much as he thought.

I got on with the reading. It was a wonderful family, full of love. Leroy eyed Jack at the beginning, but when he realized Jack would behave, he settled down and enjoyed the hour with his family.

"Well, Mrs. King, I hope that you enjoyed your time with your husband." I reached for her hand.

"I did, sweetie. You are just a doll. I'm so glad there are people like you in the world."

The rest of the family thanked me as well, and then I walked them out. After one more round of goodbyes and thank yous in the lobby, and a quick peek at Eddie, I came back to the reading room to straighten up.

"He was a tool," Jack said when I entered.

"He wasn't the only one." I looked at Jack's smug face. His expression fell.

"Me? I wasn't going to say anything. I just needed to wait for you."

"And you could have waited in a different room or place. I told you that I have to work."

"It gets boring waiting. There isn't much to do in the afterlife. I was always busy when I was alive. Creating my company, working, spending time with my wife and friends, at least until they were gone. And now, I just float around waiting on you to solve this."

I stopped picking up empty water bottles to stare at him a moment. I could understand his feelings, but it didn't give him the right to barge in on my work. My mind scrambled for the right words.

"I'm sorry, Jack. I can understand that."

"I just wish I knew what happened to me. I can't just accept that it was my time."

"Have you thought of anyone I should check out? Any possible suspect? And please don't list everyone again."

"Maybe Odette or Phyllis, also Dawn or Robin. Honestly, most of the single women at Birdsong. Not so much the married ones."

"Why?" I could guess based on Odette, Alma Jean, and Robin's brief conversation about him.

"What can I say? The ladies loved me."

"Well, if they loved you, why did they want to kill you?"

"Because they couldn't have me, and sometimes love, passion, and desire make people do stupid things."

I just had to think about Cate to know that was true. She'd killed Renee to keep her from telling anyone about her and Jeremy. Then killed Jeremy accidentally when she'd intended the victim to be Marcus, so she wouldn't have to admit that Oakley wasn't his baby but was in fact Jeremy's. It was a crazy daytime soap opera storyline, but it wasn't all that farfetched that someone would kill a person they loved.

"Alright, I'll check them all out and get back to you."

"You're sometimes hard to catch up to, but I'll be back here in a few days. Deal?"

"Deal." I smiled, and he nodded before disappearing through the wall.

There was a lot about him that reminded me of Jeremy. There was the arrogance, the business-like demeanor, and his impatience. As with Jeremy, I couldn't wait to be finished with this case. I liked my simple life without petulant ghosts.

But like Jeremy, he seemed to have a sweet, caring side as well. The one that gave me a bit of sympathy towards him and made me want to help.

Chapter Seven

I woke up early on Saturday. It was Oakley and Aspen's birthday party. Normally I wasn't a morning person, but today I jumped out of bed and flew through my morning routine before going to wake up Oakley.

"Good morning, princess!" I said, entering her beautiful gold and pink room. Her biological mother had picked out this color scheme, and to honor her, I kept it.

Someday I would update it, especially once Oakley was old enough to voice her opinion, which given how fast she was growing, wouldn't be long.

Oakley's birthday outfit was a gold and pink polka dot romper with skirt and ruffles from her waist to her knees. I would add tights and a pink sweater as it was a bit cool. Pink Mary Jane shoes completed the look.

I knew the outfit wouldn't stay clean the entire party, but as long as I managed to get some pictures for Cate, I would be happy.

Chewy could read my excitement and he bounced and spun next to me.

"Yes, it's baby girl's special day." Though her actual birthday was on Tuesday and Aspen's was Friday. "Let's get some breakfast and then we'll get you dressed for your party."

I scrambled her an egg and added a piece of toast cut into strips. Next, I added some sliced strawberries and banana. She wouldn't eat all the strawberries and banana, so I put half in a bowl and topped with some plain yogurt for myself.

I watched as she fed herself and then Chewy. The mutt never took from her plate or hand, only if she dropped it, which she did often and on purpose.

"Dawg," she said and dropped a bit of toast. He had it before it even hit the floor. She clapped.

"Okay, dog has had enough. You need to eat so we can go see your sister."

"Sissy!" She squealed.

While we ate breakfast, my cell phone chimed. My heart fluttered when I saw the display said Clint.

Sorry. I'm sure you understand but I won't be there today.

I replied that I understood, but honestly, I didn't, or at least didn't understand why he hadn't come to talk to me about it. Marriage was a huge step that we'd never even discussed, and until he asked me, I didn't know we were that serious. He really hadn't given me a good answer about why he thought we were at that point either. It left me feeling sad, lonely, and oddly vulnerable.

May I stop by tomorrow? I have a gift for Oakley, and I'd like to talk.

I stopped breathing for a moment reading that.

Yes, of course. We'll be here all day.

I looked at my daughter as she happily shoved food in her mouth and dropped another bite over the side for the dog. I didn't want her to be hurt by having him coming in and out of our lives, so I'd have to draw a line with him. Going forward, I'd be more cautious about introducing her to anyone I was dating.

I was still new to this mom thing and there was a lot to learn, not just about child development and feeding. Being a single mom had added challenges that we'd both have to figure out along the way.

"Dawg. Dawg," she pointed.

"Yes, he loves your eggs." I chuckled. "But he has his own food."

"No, no." She looked at him and said it. He seemed to frown at her words.

"Aw, come on, Chewy, why don't you go patrol the yard." I walked him to the back door. He happily went out and began his duty.

Once she was done eating, I bathed her and got her dressed in her outfit.

"Aw, sweet girl. Look at you."

She grinned. "Pi'ture?"

"Okay." I took out my camera and took a few pictures of her. She was so excited and clapped through the whole impromptu photo session. "Alright, let's go see Sissy."

"Sissy!" She clapped.

I gathered up our stuff and Aspen's gift, then loaded the baby in the car. I put on her favorite music as we drove over to her party.

I was so glad we'd catered the event. It saved us a lot of time and shopping. Also, we'd put up most of the decorations yesterday, so today was just a matter of last-minute touches and then hosting.

We were both the planned type, which meant neither of us liked to wait until the last minute, and we'd worked together well to get this party organized.

"Here we are, birthday girl."

She clapped and cheered.

Laney met us at the door with a dolled-up Aspen.

"Sissy!" They both exclaimed when they saw each other and then reached for each other. I nearly dropped Oakley and it looked like Laney was having an equally difficult time holding onto Aspen.

"Hold on, you two." Laney laughed. "Let's get you inside."

We took them to the playroom, which was set up near the living room and kitchen. There was a baby gate across the doorway so the girls could play in there safely, and we would be able to keep an eye on them while we finished setting up.

"How're you doing?" she asked as we got to work.

"I'm good. How about you?"

"I'm good, but I meant since things with Clint. We haven't talked about it again since that day at the park."

"Oh, I'm okay." I smoothed out the pink tablecloth I was holding. "He messaged me today."

"Yeah?"

"Yeah. He wants to stop by tomorrow to talk."

"That sounds promising, yes?"

"I guess. I'm not sure what he will say or what he wants to talk about, but I'm nervous."

"I can understand." Laney said, putting her hand on my arm. "So, how does the banner look?"

We looked up at the birthday banner we'd hung above the girls' highchairs. It was pastel pink, blue, and yellow letters on a mint green background.

"I think it's perfect."

We finished up with the decorating and then the caterers arrived to set up, followed quickly by party guests. Her mom, my parents, aunts, uncles, cousins, and many friends were all here to celebrate our girls with us.

When my parents and Aunt Susie arrived, Stan helped my dad

get settled as he was still on crutches.

"Do you need anything, Dad?" I said, giving him a hug once he was seated in Laney's recliner. It was perfect because he could put his leg up.

"Water?"

"Coming right up."

"And where is my granddaughter?" my mother asked.

"Harris has her in the playroom with the other kids." I pointed towards the room.

Harris was my sister's oldest son. He was six years old now and loved his baby cousin. Dylan was her youngest and was now three years old and loved his cousin too.

In fact, Harris took charge of his little cousin for the entire day, like he always did, making sure she enjoyed her first birthday. He helped her play games and was by her side during the cake smashing.

"She's so messy!" He giggled as he tried wiping her face. She turned her face away from him as she tried to grab more cake.

Aspen was just as messy, and every few seconds they would look over at each other and giggle. It was almost like they couldn't believe they were getting away with this.

Once that was done, people started to leave, but only a core group stayed to help with cleanup and visit. The girls were worn out, so once they were cleaned up, they went right down for a nap in Aspen's room.

"Go sit down, you two." Josh insisted. "Micah and I can handle cleanup."

Laney and I smiled. "Thank you both so much."

"I'll help too," Audrey said, grabbing a trash bag.

I went to sit near my parents and Aunt Susie, who had come into town just for the party. Harris was showing Mom how to play a game on Stan's phone while Dylan curled up in my dad's lap, half asleep.

"What a fun party," my dad said, smiling.

"I still can't believe our girls are one year old." I squeezed Laney's hand.

"I know. It was just yesterday that we met."

"It really feels that way."

There was a lull in the conversation. I looked towards the

kitchen to see Micah, Josh, and Audrey cleaning up. Stan and Laney's mother were taking down the party decorations for us.

"So, Dad, have you thought anymore about downsizing?" I asked.

He and my mom looked at each other, but their expressions were unreadable.

"We have, but we're just concerned about where to go or what to do next."

"I think you should check out Birdsong. I went with Laney last week and it was wonderful." I looked at her. She knew I'd planned this if the opportunity arose.

"My grandmother loves it there. She's always busy, has tons of friends, and there's always something fun going on."

With her grandmother being older than my parents, I didn't want that to be a deterrent. Many people their age lived there, though they would be some of the younger ones.

"We'll think about it," my mom said through pursed lips and a side-eye look at my father. Clearly, this had been a sore spot between my parents.

My aunt kept her mouth shut, but I could tell by her expression she'd already heard it all. I'd have to remember to call her later to ask about it.

"Anytime you're ready for a tour, I'm happy to arrange it," Laney offered with a smile.

After everything was cleaned, we loaded the gifts into my car, which we'd open at home later and send thank you cards. It was a lot to open during the party.

Stan and Micah helped Dad get into their car.

"Thank you for having us," my mom said to Laney.

"Yes, thank you," Aunt Susie said, hugging Laney.

"I'm glad you could all come." Laney said, then waved to my dad.

We stood as they drove away. Once they were out of sight, everyone else loaded up in their cars and left.

"I think it was a success," I said to Laney when it was just the two of us.

"I think it was. The perfect way to celebrate our girls." She smiled. "But, I have to admit, I'm a bit sad that Jeremy didn't show up today. I thought he might."

"I did too, but I haven't seen him in quite a while."

"That makes me oddly sad."

"To be honest, me too."

I went back inside to get Oakley. Thankfully, she stayed asleep. It was all the excitement and sugar that had her out like a light.

I was so thankful that nothing unusual or crazy had happened. It seemed like this past year had been a roller coaster ride of good, bad, and the ugly. I peeked in the backseat at one of the good.

"I love you, my sweet girl."

Chapter Eight

I'd chickened out and didn't text Joanna until Saturday, the day of Oakley's party. The Chief had not been happy that I hadn't talked to her yet, but I just told him we kept missing each other. It had worked at first, but then I think he realized I was stalling.

"Get that signed before Monday or I'll knock you down to traffic duty," he'd commanded.

"Yes, sir. Of course."

I didn't know if he really would demote me for that, but I didn't want to take my chances. I picked Saturday to text her because I knew she would be busy and would likely not want to chat much. It had only been a few messages back and forth, but I was strangely disappointed.

I wanted her to beg for me to come back. Tell me she was wrong, and we were meant to be together, like a few other girls had done. But that's the thing I liked. Joanna wasn't like other girls. There was just something different about her.

She had a spark or a bit of spunk that made her interesting. She was confident, strong, and a little bit crazy. Yet she liked to be told she was pretty and have me relocate spiders for her.

"Gah, I miss her."

I said to my ceiling as I sat on my couch. I hadn't done a thing today. Normally, I would have already gone for a morning run and then played a round or two of hoops with some of the guys at the gym.

Many Saturdays I had gone to the park with Joanna, Oakley, and Chewy. I thought of the baby's smiling face and giggle as I'd push her in the swing. She loved to swing.

My phone rang. Uncle Doug's number showed on the display.

"Hey, Uncle Doug."

"What's up, loser." His deep voice teased.

"Nothing much."

"Donna said your girl broke it off with you and that you'd likely be sulking on your couch." How did he know that? And why was my mom telling him all my secrets? "I'm in town for the weekend and thought I'd take you out. A round of golf perhaps?"

"Sure."

"Alright, I'll ask Ray and we'll likely need a fourth. Know anyone?"

"I could ask Terry, but it's the weekend, so he likely has a honey-do list or kid stuff going on." I thought about Stan, Joanna's brother-in-law.

I knew he enjoyed golf from time to time too. Was he off limits now that we'd broken up? I would try Terry first and then Stan in a pinch.

"Great. We'll be over to pick you up shortly. Be ready."

I hung up with Doug and immediately called Terry.

"Hey, Hartley, what's up?"

"Hey, bud, I know it's the weekend, but want to play a round of golf? It would be with my dad and my uncle."

"Oh, dang, I would love to, but we have track practice for Devon, viola practice for Jade, Deshawn has basketball, and little Kelvin has swim lessons at the Y."

"Wow, that's a full day."

"Yes, it's a divide-and-conquer day. I'll be lucky to get five minutes with Whitney."

"Alright, I knew it was a long shot. Enjoy."

We hung up. I stared at my phone. As I started to scroll to his contact, I remembered that Stan would be at Oakley's party, so he was out. Perhaps someone out of the box would be the way to go.

I hit the number before I changed my mind.

"Hello?"

"Hey, Eddie. It's Clint, uh, Hartley."

"Oh, hey, man. What's up?"

"You don't happen to play golf, do you?"

"Hell, yeah I do!"

I asked him to meet me at my house. After I gave him the address, I sprinted to get dressed before my uncle and dad arrived.

An hour later, we pulled into a spot at Creekview Country Club. I should have thought this through more before inviting Eddie to an outing with my Chief of Police uncle, but thankfully Eddie knew how to play this game.

"So, Eddie, what do you do?" Doug asked as we got set up at the first tee.

I cringed. I hoped Eddie didn't give too much information to my Chief of Police uncle. Doug might not be as tolerant of what we let Hank and his men get away with here.

"I'm a security manager for Hammersley Property Management."

"You work security or security?" Doug knew exactly what Eddie did then. There was no fooling him.

"I manage the security team that provides guards to our properties. I also oversee the cameras and our IT department who monitors them," Eddie said firmly so there were no more questions.

But Doug being Doug, "Is that how you two know each other then? You provide footage when needed?"

We looked at each other. Basically, but I think we first met because of Hank's other businesses. Eddie wasn't doing security back then. I was a beat cop, and he was still doing debt enforcement. We'd had a few run-ins, but over time we'd formed a bond. Maybe it was because we both wanted Joanna and Oakley safe.

"Yes, he's been extremely helpful on a number of cases," I said. Eddie nodded.

I then stepped up to take my turn before Doug asked much more. I didn't want to have to explain our whole strange relationship. I'd have to explain why we sometimes looked the other way when it came to Hank. His business was mostly legal, so it wasn't completely unethical.

We played through about four holes before the beer cart caught up to us.

"This round's on me," Eddie said.

We all thanked him and placed our order. The beer was perfectly cold, and the day was gorgeous. Though it was an odd foursome, it was still shaping up to be a good day.

"So, Clint, what's up with you and your girl?" Doug asked while we waited for the team ahead to play through.

"What can I say? We broke up."

Eddie whipped his head around. "You and Jo broke up?"

"Um, yeah," I said, my voice cracking. "I asked her to marry me, and she said no."

"Seriously? That's harsh." Eddie said. He put an arm around my shoulders. "I'm sorry, man."

"You asked her to marry you? I didn't know you were that serious with her," my dad said. "Does your mom know?"

"No, she doesn't. I guess we weren't. I think I just got caught up in the moment."

"What moment? Like sex?" Doug said with a chuckle.

"No, not then. We'd just solved a big case, and I was on an adrenaline high."

"You had a ring with you?" he asked.

"Well, no."

"Had you at least talked about getting married?"

"Also, no." Maybe she was right. We weren't ready. "Gosh, I had thought..."

Man, I had a lot of apologizing to do. Maybe we could still salvage things. I'd never been really good at communicating, but she hadn't either, or perhaps I wasn't a good listener.

We finished up the rest of the holes without talking about me again. We kept the conversation on sports and work, mostly. Then after we'd finished, we headed to the clubhouse to grab a late lunch and a few more beers.

"So, Ray, you'll be retiring soon?" Doug asked his brother.

"Yep, yep. Very soon."

"What are you going to do with yourself?"

"Donna has a lot of plans for me. Mostly involving traveling."

"You hate traveling," Doug chuckled.

"Yeah, but she doesn't, and happy wife, happy life."

None of the rest of us were married, so we just laughed along but didn't reply.

"And how about you, kid? Any interesting cases you can talk about?" Doug asked me.

"Um, not really. Just the normal fare. We had a home invasion recently and a murder-suicide. Then I'm waiting on an autopsy for an old guy over at one of our senior communities, but I'm expecting it to be a heart attack or something else related to age. What about you?"

"About the same, though quieter since you helped us with the Redlynne gang."

"Well, that was a lot to do with Joanna. She pointed me in the right direction."

"Either way, it helped. Has your department thought about

using her as a consultant?"

"Funny you should ask that. Yes, and I'm supposed to be the one to talk to her about it."

"How did you get so lucky?" Doug asked.

"I guess I pissed off karma or something."

"Do you think she'll say yes to that?" Eddie asked, but then quickly added, "Sorry, man, not a shot at the marriage thing. It was an innocent question."

"No problem, and honestly, I have no idea what she'll say."

We wrapped up the meal shortly after that. Doug drove us first to my house since that's where Eddie's truck was.

"Thanks for the distraction today," I said to my uncle.

He hadn't always been my favorite person, but we'd come to an understanding during the Redlynne gang investigation.

"Anytime, nephew." He hugged me.

I waved to my dad. Eddie stayed for a moment after they drove off.

"So, hey, full disclosure. I asked Joanna out a few weeks ago. It was a slip in judgment, and honestly it was just for coffee, but I'd felt bad about it since."

"Oh, um, what did she say?" I was trying not to overreact, but I wanted to punch his face. However, knowing his strength and respecting his honesty with me, I held myself in check.

"She said no. I haven't asked her again." He looked down. "I'm sorry. It wasn't meant as a romantic thing exactly, but kind of."

"I'm not thrilled about it, but truth be told, she and I apparently weren't as close as I thought."

"I just feel better telling you." He took a few steps towards his truck. "Well, thanks for asking me today. I needed to get out, and I haven't played golf in a while, not since..." He quickly turned and left.

I watched him leave, wondering what the heck that last part meant, but then decided not to give it a lot of brain power because it was likely Hank business. Best to just turn a blind eye to that. If there were no bodies or visible crime, it was just better I didn't know, at least for today.

Chapter Nine

~ Joanna ~

I woke up this morning with an ache in my stomach.

Clint was coming. That was my first thought before my feet even touched the floor.

It had been several weeks since I'd seen him and turned down his proposal. Even now the shock of the moment filled me with panic.

I lay in bed staring at my wall. My boring wall without any artwork, only a window that looked out the side of my house at a three-foot strip of grass and then my privacy fence. Though at the moment, the blinds were still pulled and the curtains drawn. There was no point in opening them since I couldn't see anything anyway.

"How can I face him today?"

Hearing my voice, Chewy gave a quick, soft bark and trotted over to me. He greeted me with a smile, his always wagging tail, and a bunch of puppy kisses on my face.

"Aw, I love you too, Chewy-boy." I sat up. "Want to go out?"

He barked and spun around, then ran towards my bedroom door. I padded over and opened it. He darted out and straight to the back door. I chuckled when I caught up to him.

"You're much faster than me," I said as I opened the back door. He ran out into the dark yard.

I left the door cracked, knowing he would come back in when he was done, and no, I didn't worry about someone getting in as long as he was around. He'd proven time and again that he would at least try to protect us.

I turned back into the kitchen, heading straight to the coffee pot. I added a pod and a mug, then pushed the button. While that ran, I went to the bathroom.

With that done, I met Chewy back in the kitchen.

"Ready for some food?"

While he ate, I sat watching him and thinking about the day ahead.

I wasn't sure what time Clint was planning to come over, but I had no plans to go anywhere. I was going to open Oakley's gifts and write thank you cards, then I'd probably read and answer any fan emails between caring for and playing with her.

But for the next hour until it was time to get the baby up, I had nothing much to do, so I thought about Jack Reynolds and Birdsong. I hadn't spoken to him in a few days.

He hadn't come back yet after giving me those few names of women to look into. I had yet to do much with them either. I wasn't sure how to go about it. Maybe when I did the group reading on Friday, I could find out more about them.

But after having lunch with Odette, I just didn't see her as the type. I was curious to find out more about the hussy in 1143 and meet her.

Since I'd already met Odette and Robin, that left Phyllis and Dawn, at least out of the names Jack had given me. I had to hope that whoever it was showed up to the group reading.

Chewy finished his breakfast, so he headed back outside to patrol his yard. I started a new cup of coffee and then headed into the living room where the mountain of gifts was located. I set my mug down.

This felt overwhelming. I probably should have told people no gifts. Oakley needed almost nothing. She had everything a toddler could ask for. But I was happy that so many people loved her and wanted to celebrate her life.

Between her and Aspen, we had over a hundred people at their party. Not all guests brought a gift for both girls as some were solely for us or only there for Aspen. It had been perfect though.

"Well, these aren't going to open themselves." And Oakley was still a bit young to fully get it. I'd already tried with her, but it turned into more of a photo session than progress towards getting these opened. So the job of opening fell to me.

Chewy had joined me and was watching in case I had something for him.

"Okay, first gift. From Janie." At her name, Chewy's ears perked. "Sorry, boy."

She'd given Oakley a toddler puzzle and a spring outfit. I wrote it on the list. Then moved to the next gift from Tessa, Ruby, and Elsa. With each gift, I smiled and wrote it down. Most were new clothes, which was perfect. She'd started to outgrow her current things, and we were only a month or so away from the season changing. With all these new outfits, she would be the best-dressed toddler.

I continued opening until Oakley woke and I went to get her up and changed, then fixed her breakfast. While I watched her eat, my phone chimed.

My pulse quickened, thinking it was Clint, but it was Al.

I wanna bring a gift later. Time?

Anytime. We're home all day.

K

It was going to be a busy day of guests. I looked over at my daughter as she shoveled a piece of pancake into her mouth, followed by a chunk of blueberry, followed quickly by a piece of pancake on the floor for Chewy.

I couldn't help but think what might have happened to her had she gone into the foster system when Cate was taken to jail. I visibly shuddered at the thought.

But we'd both been blessed with the option for me to adopt her, and now look at our lives. She had so many people who wanted to celebrate her and a pile of gifts in the living room.

My phone chimed again, interrupting my thought. This time it was Clint.

Do you have time now?

I took a deep breath before replying.

Yes

Two seconds later, my doorbell rang. Oh, he really meant now.

I looked at the baby in her highchair. She would be fine for a moment, and I could see her from the front door. Chewy barked and spun his way to the door.

I opened it to find Clint. He smiled, but his eyes didn't quite tell the same story. They looked sad and empty.

"Hi. I didn't realize you meant now-now," I said with a laugh.

"Oh, I... I'm sorry. Want me to come back?"

"No, no. Just, why don't you come in?"

He nodded and stepped in. Chewy bounced around him.

"Hey, who's a good boy?" Clint said, petting the dog with one hand. In his other he held an envelope and a gift bag. "Oh, before I forget."

He passed me the gift bag with a puppy on it. He shoved the

envelope into his pocket.

"Thank you." I took it and set it on the coffee table. But the oddness of the envelope had me curious.

"Da! Da!" Oakley started yelling and kicking in her chair when she saw him.

"Hi, sweet girl. What do you have there?"

She held up a blueberry for him to see and then popped it in her mouth. He smiled, then turned to me. He took me in with a simple glance.

"You look good."

"Oh, thanks." I actually didn't feel cute.

My hair was up in a messy bun. I was wearing some bleach-stained sweatpants with an oversized, out-of-shape t-shirt. "Would you like some coffee?"

"Sure. Thanks."

I got an extra mug out. It was a dark blue one with yellow stripes that he used all the time when he stayed here. Since we'd broken up, I couldn't bring myself to use it.

I popped in a pod for him and then we waited in tense silence for his coffee. The dog had plopped down at Clint's feet and Oakley was chattering and eating.

When his coffee was ready, I set the mug in front of him.

"Thanks." He mumbled. He cleared his throat. "Um, so, the chief wanted me to ask you about something."

"The chief as in your boss, the chief of police?"

"Yes." He paused. "Terry had this idea, and he approached the chief with it, and I guess it was decided or discussed. They want to see if you'll be a consultant for us."

I had no idea what that meant, and the request caught me off guard. A million thoughts ran through my mind.

"A consultant? What's that mean exactly?"

"Well, you would help us out on homicide cases, basically like you have been with the Landon case, the Playhouse killer. You know?" He handed me the crumpled envelope from his pocket. "Sorry, I probably shouldn't have folded it. That's the offer letter."

"Wow, just wow." I sat back with a thud as I took the envelope from him but didn't open it. Mystery solved of the secret envelope.

I didn't know how to answer this. I did like doing the investigations, but it wasn't something I would have chosen to do.

This had just found me in the form of Jeremy Landon. Of course, I didn't know how I'd gotten my psychic powers initially, just born with them, and never figured out how I'd gotten them back either.

I stared at the envelope for a moment, then looked up at him.

"What do you think about me doing it? And how would that work? Would I be working with you and Terry?"

"Well, I don't know exactly, but yes, you'd work with Terry and me, plus the other two detectives, Jackson and Simmons. You remember Andrea Jackson, right?"

"Yes, I do. I like her." I nodded. I hadn't met the other one yet, but I'd met Andrea Jackson once. "Would you be okay working with me?"

He stared, seeming to study me, but he didn't speak right away. I tried not to fidget under his intense stare.

"Honestly, I would. I can, but no matter what, I just want you to be safe," he finally said.

"I'll definitely consider the offer. I'm just not sure how much time I have to give to it and my business and of course Oakley."

"That's understandable." He looked at her.

"Do you know how long I have to consider it?"

"I think it's in the offer letter."

"Alright then. I'll look it over and give you a call when I decide, I guess?"

"Yes, that works."

We sat there silently again. He sipped the coffee and looked at Oakley. My phone rang. It was Josh.

"Oh, well, I'll let you get on with your day." He stood, then touched the baby's head. "Happy birthday, baby girl."

"Clint?" I let the phone ring. I could call Josh back.

"Yes?" He turned towards me.

I had no idea what I wanted to say to him. I just didn't want him to leave yet. I looked around for any excuse to keep him here.

"Why don't you stay while I open the gift for her?" I smiled.

He smiled softly and nodded towards my phone. "What about Josh?"

"I can call him back."

Our eyes locked, holding for a moment before he took a seat again.

I picked up the gift and pulled out the soft, crinkly tissue paper, then peered into the bag. Inside was a cute berry-colored all-cotton romper. It had a bow tied around the waist, but it was sewn on, so no chance that little miss could untie it. Also in the bag were some matching moccasins.

"These are super cute." Then I realized there was more in the bag hiding under a second layer of paper. I pulled out a can of tennis balls and immediately burst into laughter. "So she can play with Chewy."

"Yes! Exactly. A gift for them both." He patted the mutt's head.

"Thank you for this. They'll have fun, and this outfit is really cute." I fought the urge to hug him.

"I can't take all the credit for the outfit. My mom helped." He smiled the first genuine smile. "I just knew her size."

"Will you tell her it's perfect?"

"I will." He said, and then he stood again. "Just let Terry or me know your decision about the job, okay?"

"Sure."

I walked him to the door. He looked at me with tears in his eyes but didn't say anything. He simply nodded, then walked to his truck. I stood there watching him drive away. I felt that crushing pain in my chest like the day I turned him down.

How was I going to work with him? I'd figure it out because even though it was crazy, I was seriously considering taking them up on their offer.

Chapter Ten

I smiled as I parked in front of our office on Monday morning. Like many mornings, I would sit in the car for a moment looking at the building with the perfectly manicured landscaping.

When Hank had presented this opportunity, it had been the perfect fit. Smiling, I grabbed my purse, which had the offer letter from Chief Ortiz.

I'd tossed and turned all night thinking about what I'd say or do. Did I want to consult with the police department? Would it mean giving up time here?

I knew that last question might be silly as I hadn't given up much time doing both with my last investigations, even though to date, I hadn't officially been consulting for the department. It had just been a thing I did to help some spirits who needed me.

It also wasn't foolproof. Not every ghost came to see me. Not all of them felt like their business on Earth was unfinished. If they did, my world would be a lot more crowded.

Though that didn't help me decide what to do in this situation.

I sighed.

Maybe I should discuss it with Micah and Tessa.

They'd always been my sounding boards, especially Micah. He'd helped me start this business and had been with me since day one. Tessa came along soon after and quickly became one of my best friends.

"Are you going to stand out here all day?" Micah called with a laugh from the front door.

"Ha, sorry, I was lost in thought."

I jogged over and he held the door wide for me.

"Thanks, and good morning," I said, stepping inside.

"Good morning to you, and nice of you to finally join us." He teased. "We can't do this without you."

I looked over at the security guard desk. Today we had Percy back. Thank goodness.

"Good morning, Percy. How are you today?"

"I'm well, Ms. Joanna, and how are you?"

"Doing well." I smiled and then joined my assistants at the reception desk. "Schedule?"

"In your chair. No messages yet."

"Perfect." I then turned to Micah. "Status on our order?"

"Should be here today."

"Great." I paused. Did I really want to bring them in on this? Yes. "Do y'all have a second to chat? In my office?"

"Sure." They both said.

"Percy, can you keep an eye on things? I'll be right back," Tessa added.

"Sure thing, Ms. Tessa."

We headed to my office. I threw my purse into my desk, but I pulled the letter out before closing the drawer. Then I waited for them to settle.

"Okay, so, Clint came to see me yesterday."

"Really? Why?" Micah asked as he sat forward.

"Well, for one, he brought Oakley a gift since, obviously, he didn't come to the party and, well, you know?" They nodded. "But also, he said that they'd like me to work as a consultant for the police department." I passed the letter across the desk. Micah took it and held it so Tessa could see it.

"Like on murder cases?" Tessa asked. I nodded. "Oh, interesting."

"Yeah. But I don't know what to say. Should I do it?"

"What about this business?"

"Well, I should be able to do it still. Those past investigations didn't get too much in the way of working here. Maybe I might do one less appointment a day or something, but it should be doable."

They looked at each other. We'd already agreed to not do another tour for a while, so that shouldn't be a problem, but I knew they were likely worried about their own jobs. Completely understandable.

"What would we do while you are doing that, boss?"

"Well, I hope you would continue to work with me. I mean, we've had some fun times chasing leads, I thought."

"Not that time we got locked in the building with a dead body." He gagged.

"Oh, yes, that was awful. Like rotting fish and cabbage." A full body shudder went through me.

"I'm glad I missed that one," Tessa said.

"Yeah, you did not miss a thing," Micah said.

"Alright, so what did we decide? Am I doing this?"

"I vote for yes, boss."

"Me too."

"Well then, it's settled. Joanna the medium with a heart is now also a consultant for the Creekview Police Department." Micah handed me the letter back. I took a deep breath, then signed it. "Done. I'll call, I guess Clint, later to tell him."

"Exciting!" Tessa said.

"I can't wait for the first case." Micah rubbed his hands together.

"Actually, I have been approached by a spirit and I've looked into it a tiny bit." I thought for a moment. "I guess I should tell Terry and Clint because they're likely expecting this to come back as natural causes."

"Who? Who?" Micah blurted out during my thinking out loud.

"Jack Reynolds. He was that guy they recently reported on the news that died at Birdsong."

"Ah, now it makes sense! You're doing the reading so quickly because of his death and what you might learn from it."

"Bingo. But also because of my parents. I really think they need to downsize, and this place really sounds like their type of place."

"Despite the possible murder?" Tessa laughed.

"Of course, without that part."

"Are we going with you to the reading, boss?"

"I hadn't thought about it, but now that you mention it, you probably both should be there. Just like when we're on tour."

They both said they would, and we agreed on details for Friday. It was getting close to our first appointment time, so we broke up our meeting after that.

I did my usual prep things before the clients arrived, which left me no time to send Clint a text message. I'd have to do it between my appointments.

As it turned out, it wasn't until around lunchtime before I had a spare minute to text him.

I've decided to accept the offer. Now what?

While I waited for his reply, I pulled up my internet browser and decided to do a little research on the ladies of Birdsong.

I sat there a moment with the blinking cursor mocking me as I tried to decide where to start.

"These ladies likely aren't on social media, or not much," I mumbled. "But maybe..."

I typed in Birdsong and found all their social media. There were tons of pictures and posts about their various activities and parties. Kelli was right. She definitely tried to give everyone good memories.

I found an album of all the craft projects, including the birdhouses they'd been working on the day I was there. There were a few pictures with each of the proud decorators and then a few of them hung in the trees. They all turned out great.

There were watercolors, painting pottery, gardening, various seasonal crafts. They did a lot of projects, or at least they had a lot of pictures of them.

"Mom would love this part."

As I was clicking, I saw they had them labeled with residents' names. I saw a group shot with the names Phyllis, Dawn, Margo, and Karen. I at least knew who Margo was. She was the shortest one with the pink colored hair. But I tried to find one of just Phyllis or just Dawn without luck. They were always in group shots.

I found some of Alma Jean and her friends, and of course I'd met Odette, so I knew her right away. I'd have to wait until I got to Birdsong on Friday and hoped that they both were in the audience.

If I got the chance, I'd try to talk to them individually, even if briefly, get a feel for them. I'd also try to bring up Jack.

But I had no idea how many were planning to attend and if I'd get a chance to have one-on-one conversations. It would be harder to ask with others around.

I pushed the X on the browser and just stared at the wallpaper. It was an old picture of Chewy sitting next to Oakley in her highchair. It was taken when she was first old enough to sit up in it. It always made me smile.

My phone chimed.

I can swing by your office to pick it up.

Sounds good. We are here until 4.

Great

Now it would really be official, and I'd have to tell him about Jack. I was a bit nervous about that. He wouldn't like me withholding information, but it wasn't like I'd had an obligation, until now, to tell him.

I ran up to reception to let Tessa know that Clint was on his way.

"I'm excited!" She gushed. "I loved helping with these in the past. I hate that we didn't get to do more with the Senator's case."

"I know. I would have liked to have dived more into that one, but to be honest, I'd had quite enough of the Crawfords."

"Well, do you want me to send him back or buzz you when he gets here?"

"Both?"

"Got it."

I went back to get ready for my last appointment and then wait nervously for Clint to show up.

I greeted the Huangs. They were here to connect with their daughter. She'd passed away a few months ago. I'd already spoken to her, and she was waiting here for them to arrive.

"I'm a bit nervous to talk to them again," Iris said as she paced around the reading room while I put out water and ensured I had enough tissues.

"It will be fine. I've done enough of these to know whatever happened during life doesn't matter much now."

"I hope so. They weren't happy with my life choices. They wanted me to be a doctor, but instead I worked as a stunt woman."

"Wow, stunt woman sounds exciting."

"It was until it wasn't. That's how I died."

"Oh my. I'm sorry."

"Meh, it happened. My partner wasn't being careful and bam, we both lost our grip. Fell."

"Did your partner die too?"

"No, but his stunt days are over. He has slight paralysis, mostly his left side."

By the time her parents had arrived, I had all the drama and was ready for whatever happened. Thankfully, it was how I expected.

The parents missed her and were proud of her, despite their earlier hopes.

"You were wonderful at your job," Mrs. Huang said.

"We couldn't have been prouder of you," Mr. Huang said, wiping a tear.

It was a beautiful reading, and I was riding that high as I waited for Clint. My nervous energy had me cleaning as I paced between my office, the reading room, and the break room. They were nearly spotless when he finally arrived.

I missed Tessa buzzing my office as I was in the break room, and he came walking down the hallway. Our eyes locked. My knees felt weak, but I managed a smile.

"Hey, Clint."

"Hey." He nodded.

His stoic expression was nearly unreadable, which had me brushing back a strand of hair behind my ear and thinking this was all a huge mistake. How was I going to work with him?

"I have the signed offer on my desk." I gestured for him to follow me.

Stepping in, I could smell the faint scent of the orange cleaner I'd been using. It was calming, which was what I needed right now.

"Here you go." I handed it to him.

He took it and looked it over for a bit longer than was necessary, but then he glanced at me.

"Great. I'm looking forward to our first case."

"Well, now that you mention it..."

"You already have something?"

"You know Jack Reynolds who used to live at Birdsong?"

"And let me guess, he says he's been murdered but has no proof?" His sarcastic tone wasn't lost on me.

"It seems you already know, but yes." I tried to match his tone.

"It's a pattern with you."

"But I've gotten results, haven't I?"

"At what cost?" He snapped. I crossed my arms but didn't answer, so he continued. "Nearly your life several times."

I couldn't argue with that even though I wanted to. It was the same argument we'd had several times already.

"Well, for what it's worth, I haven't gotten much done with investigating yet as he only came to me about a week ago."

He sighed and pinched the bridge of his nose.

"Okay, well, I'm currently waiting on the autopsy results, so when I get those, I'll let you know." He said, some of the steam gone from his tone. "What're your next steps?"

"I have a group reading scheduled at Birdsong for this Friday, so I'm hoping to find something more then."

"Like what?"

"Well, he gave me a couple of names, so I'm going to see if I can at least meet them while doing the reading. Nothing more, and if there seems to be anything, I will let you know."

He stared at me for a moment, his expression flat. The saying if looks could kill flashed through my mind.

"I guess that's safe enough for now. Just please think about Oakley, your parents, and your sister before charging into things."

I simply nodded, biting my tongue and not wanting to remind him that caution hadn't kept me safe from Vera. But I needed him on my side with this, so I let it go.

"Well, I'll get this back to the station. Please let me know if you find anything." He started to walk out, then stopped. "I talked to Eddie recently. Actually, we went to play a round of golf with my uncle and dad over the weekend."

"Oh yeah?" I tried not to show my surprise.

"Yeah, he mentioned about asking you for coffee a few weeks ago?" He chuckled. "I guess I'm not the only one you turn down."

"Clint, I'm sorry. You caught me off guard that day."

"No, I'm sorry. I shouldn't have, I shouldn't have assumed we were in the same place, and I realize that now."

We stood there in silence for a moment, looking at anything but each other.

He broke the silence. "I didn't mean to start this. I really need to get this back to the station, but maybe we can chat about things, us, soon?"

"I'd like that."

I walked him to the lobby and watched him go out the front door. Only after he left could I fully breathe. My reaction to him had me second-guessing my decision to work with him, but I'd already agreed, so I was stuck now.

Plus, I'd made a promise to Jack to help him find his killer, even though he didn't have any idea who it was or if he was really murdered. But I honored my commitments, and that was my plan, both to Jack and the Creekview Police Department.

Chapter Eleven

Tessa, Micah, and I had agreed to drive over together. We were loading Micah's car with various products, like shirts, mugs, and keychains. Things we thought they'd like.

Tessa had called Kelli this morning to get a rough idea of what we should plan on.

"Our room only holds about sixty people, so that's how many we had to limit the event to. We had a full list within minutes of announcing the event! We had to offer a waitlist, just in case," Kelli gushed.

To err on the side of caution, we'd bring enough for about eighty people. It meant we would blow through a lot of our stock, but Micah had already placed another order for us. People liked to have souvenirs from their readings.

"So, while we're there, keep an eye or ear out for Odette, Phyllis, or Dawn. Those are the names that Jack gave me," I said as we drove over. "I have met Odette, but I didn't really learn much. And I use the word suspect loosely. Jack seems wishy-washy on this suspect list."

"Sounds good, boss."

"What are we looking for, exactly?" Tessa asked.

"I don't know, but just if something seems off? Or if they say something that seems suspicious."

"I was also thinking if others are gossiping about them, that's what I was going to pay attention to," Micah added.

"That's a good idea," Tessa said.

"Also, I'm not sure how we'll find out, but Odette and the others kept mentioning someone they referred to as the hussy in 1143. I don't think we'll be able to ask about the hussy, but if you hear anyone mention either the apartment or refer to someone that way, listen carefully for the name."

They agreed.

We arrived, and I pointed Micah towards the visitor parking. We then unloaded our goodies onto our cart, then made our way to the office.

"Good afternoon, Joanna! We're so excited to have you back

with us," Velda said.

"I'm excited too."

We handed over our IDs and waited for our badges.

"I'll have Kelli come get y'all. Give me a moment." She picked up the phone. "They're here. Yes? Okay." She hung up and turned towards us. "She'll be right here."

"Thanks, Velda." While we stood there, I noticed a few spirits. One of the women stepped forward.

"Can you pass along a message for me?" she asked. I nodded. "Can you tell her Hazel is here and that I miss her?"

"Um, Velda, Hazel is here and says she misses you."

Velda's eyes misted up. She grabbed a tissue. "She is?" I nodded. "Hazel, my love, are you really here?"

"I am, darling. I have been with you since the day I passed. I'm so sorry you had to go through all of that alone. The backlash from our families while grieving. You are truly amazing."

"I did it because I had to, but oh, I'm so glad to know I wasn't alone, even though I felt so lonely."

"I plan to be with you as long as is possible. I don't know how this afterlife thing works, but I'm here." Hazel smiled at me as I spoke her words.

"I love you, Hazel."

"I love you, Velda."

"Oh, thank you, Joanna. Can I hug you?" Velda said, stepping around the desk.

"Of course." We were hugging as Kelli came inside.

"I feel like I missed something big in here," Kelli said with a laugh.

"Joanna here was giving me love from Hazel." Velda wiped her eyes again.

"Oh, that's wonderful, Velda. I'm so happy for you." Kelli stepped forward and hugged her. Then she turned to me. "Ready? We're going to have a packed house!"

"I'm excited." I then turned. "By the way, this is my team, Micah and Tessa."

"Oh, nice to meet you both and put a face to the voice, Tessa." She smiled, thrusting her hand out to each of them. "Can I help you with anything?"

"I think we've got it, but thank you," Tessa said.

I waved to Velda as we followed Kelli out and into the same courtyard that only a few weeks ago I'd stepped into for the first time. Today when I stepped into that courtyard, I was greeted by my own face on a poster.

"Oh, wow, that's me." I smiled at it.

"Yeah, I hope you don't mind. It was a good way to advertise. Not that I really needed it."

As we walked, I could hear the murmur of a crowd close by.

"I'm so glad you were able to do that reading for Velda. She's such a sweet lady, but her life was Hazel, especially after her family disowned her," Kelli said.

"Why?" I could guess, but I hated to assume.

"Their relationship. When they came out to their families, most couldn't accept it. Velda's mother wouldn't talk to her."

"Oh."

"Yeah, she passed away without speaking to her daughter again. It broke Velda."

That made me sad for them. To not be able to be your true self among the people who are supposed to love you most. I once had to hide parts of myself from my mother too. So I understood, though it was a different type of thing. The feelings of betrayal were likely the same.

As we turned the corner towards the community room, we were met with cheers and applause from those both alive and dead. Though I was the only one to know about the latter.

"Joanna!"

"She's here!"

"Hello, everyone. Thank you for coming," I said as we walked past them and into the room.

They hadn't yet let people inside, which was good for us, but seeing that many were using walkers or canes made me concerned about them standing outside. The ones in mobile scooters would be fine though.

Thankfully it wasn't warm, and they were in the shade. Still, we'd have to work quickly to ensure they could come in soon.

The room was simple. There were rows of stacking banquet chairs in various jewel tone colors. They were all facing a slightly raised area. Not tall enough to be called a stage or require any steps, but just tall enough to be a tripping hazard if you weren't paying attention.

On the right side against the wall was a six-foot table with chairs, as we'd requested. That's where we would set up our giveaways.

Kelli brought me a wireless lapel microphone, and I got that attached while Micah and Tessa set up the table. I did a quick mic check and then we were ready to have people come in. I was sure they were as anxious as I was to get this going.

I positioned myself near the door so I could greet people as they came in.

"Welcome. Hi. Nice to see you," I said as the residents poured in.

They all smiled. Some wanted to hug me or shake my hand, a simple connection. I could see the hope gleaming in their eyes. They all yearned to receive a message. I would try to get to as many as possible.

As everyone got seated, I adjusted the mic on my collar, then smoothed the front of my brown draped dress and wide belt. I'd ditched my usual stage clothing as it felt too much for the setting.

Instead, I thought the simple dress paired with a beige, loose-fitting cardigan and knee-high leather boots worked. A single strand of pearls around my neck finished the look.

I tapped the mic lightly, causing a bit of static to travel the airwaves of the room. The audience quieted.

"Hello, all. Thank you for having me out today." I nodded towards Kelli. She beamed and nodded in reply. "I know you're all hopeful to receive messages from loved ones, and I'll try to get to as many of you as I'm able to with the time we have. If I'm not able to, please see my assistants before you leave." I gestured to them, and they waved to the crowd. "We can get you scheduled for a free session, but only if you schedule with us today."

They cheered. I looked around and saw so many spirits standing among the crowd. I hadn't done a reading quite like this, so I decided on the spot how I'd handle it.

"If I can ask the spirits here today to line up here in an orderly fashion," I gestured to my right, "then I will start with the first in line and go through as many as I can. Each person will get a quick message, maybe one to two minutes."

There was a murmur through the living people in the crowd as they processed what I'd said. I then watched as the loved ones moved through the crowd, sometimes through the people, and lined up as I'd stated. I smiled at them as they took their spot.

"Alright, let's see. First up we have Wayne Carpenter. Is Denise in the audience?"

A woman in hot pink leggings with matching colored hair and a sweatshirt that said "Hot Granny" stood. She was adorable, but I still fought against a giggle.

"I'm Denise. Wayne was my second husband." Her eyes glistened with love and a few tears. Someone passed her a tissue. She thanked them and then turned back to me.

"He says he loves you and you made the last years of his life wonderful and fun. He enjoyed every minute."

"Oh, Wayne, me too. I loved you so much."

"I will be here next to you until you join me here," I said for Wayne, then thanked them and moved to the next person.

When I got to Odette, I smiled at her.

I hesitated to say her husband's words, but as people were watching me, I had to.

"Odette, I know you have been dating other men since I passed."

A gasp went through the crowd along with a few giggles mixed in. Some ladies to the right side elbowed each other and pointed. Laney was right. They loved the drama here.

"I'm sorry, Dave." Her voice wavered as a blush formed on her face. "But we did talk about that before."

"I know. It's okay. I just wanted you to know that I'm glad you are doing things for you."

She grinned and sat quickly. Nothing super crazy that would lead me to think she was a killer. Darn, maybe this wasn't going to give me anything to go on.

"Next up, we have Leroy King. Is there a Phyllis here?" I almost choked when I realized the name. Was it our Phyllis?

A murmur went through the crowd, and I noticed a few of the ladies elbow each other. A woman in her early seventies, maybe, stood, but she dressed like a twenty-something. Ripped jeans, a Rolling Stones tee with a bright red cardigan over it, and wearing black Converse. Her silver hair was cut in a stylish bob. She was stunning.

"I'm Phyllis." She flashed a weak smile and tried to avoid eye contact with the people around her.

"Oh, my Phyl, I loved you so much."

"I loved you too, Leroy. We had a wonderful fifty-five years together."

The crowd softly whispered and the gossipy ladies, as I'd started to refer to them, elbowed each other again and smirked. I was starting to really dislike them, but I already liked Phyllis. I could almost feel she had a fun energy about her.

"The kids and I talk about you almost daily," she said.

"I know. I love hearing all the fun memories between y'all." He smiled as I spoke his words.

"Well, that's all the time we have," I said when I was done with Phyllis' reading. "As I said, please see us after this if we didn't get to you today. We will schedule you for a free reading. Thank you all so much for having us."

The audience applauded and cheered, including the spirits. They thanked me. I wished I could get Leroy to wait so I could have an excuse to talk to Phyllis, but unfortunately, I couldn't.

Kelli jogged over to me, throwing her arms around me. "That was so amazing. Thank you for coming."

"You're welcome. That was fun." I turned off the microphone and handed it to her. I looked over at the line that had formed in front of Tessa and Micah. They were smiling and laughing with the residents. "My staff seems to be enjoying themselves as well."

"We would love to have y'all back anytime."

"We'd love that too, and actually I'm going to talk to Velda about getting my parents a tour here."

"Oh, that's awesome. When you do, stop by and see me. I will tell them about all the activities and fun stuff we do here."

"They will love that."

Kelli went to talk to some of the residents. I saw her hugging a few who still had tears in their eyes. I wanted to rush over and hug them too, but it didn't feel right. I was a more reserved hugger.

I turned to join my assistants but was stopped by Odette.

"It's so good to see you again, Ms. Joanna," she said, hugging me.

"It's nice to see you again. I hope you enjoyed your message."

"Oh, I did, but I felt almost busted by him. I didn't know he was around. What did he see me do?" She blushed, then waved as she walked away.

What did that mean? Just the dating or something more? I made a mental note.

Chapter Twelve

~ Clint ~

Saturday morning, I was up early and stretching for my morning run when my cell phone rang. It was Terry.

"Hey, what's up?"

"Death at Birdsong. Suspicious."

"Want me to meet you there or will you pick me up?"

"I'm heading your way in just a sec. Putting on my shoes right now."

"Alright. I'll be ready."

We hung up. I looked at my phone for a split second, then sighed. I'd been looking forward to my run. It had been a long work week, and it just got a bit longer. I needed to burn some steam.

Even though Walden said it was suspicious, we'd rarely been called there for a murder. Likely it was just a distraught family member who hadn't expected the death.

However, I would do my job and prove it if it was. Whatever it took to bring peace to the family.

Also, given what Joanna had told me about Jack claiming he was murdered, I had to have a different mindset going into this one.

I headed to my room, stripping out of my workout clothes and trading them for my usual solid-colored polo. Today was navy blue, paired with khakis. I slipped on my leather sneakers. Grabbed my badge, keys, wallet, and service piece, then shoved my cell phone in my pocket before heading outside to meet my partner.

After only a few minutes, he pulled up to the curb. I hopped in and we were off.

"So, what do we know?" I asked.

"Male, eighty-six. Found this morning by a staff member when he didn't show up at his usual breakfast time."

"Why do they think it's suspicious?"

"Honestly, they didn't say, just that he hadn't been sick or anything that they were aware of."

"I guess we'll see when we get there."

We drove in near silence, then when we arrived, followed the patrol officer's instructions to drive around through the resident entrance. She was keeping the media outside the gates.

This was a bit different. Usually, we just checked in at the front office and were let in. Between that and the media presence, it had me intrigued about what we would find.

"How do they always find out so quickly?" I mumbled.

"Probably a nosy neighbor called this one in," Terry answered.

I nodded. That was likely true.

"This is being handled a bit different than the others we've been here for," Terry said as he parked near the victim's unit.

"Yeah, I was just thinking the same, and it looks like a lot of officers today. Strange."

We headed in to meet the officer in charge. Officer Woods and Martinez were controlling the scene. We nodded to them as we went into the apartment.

"Body?" I asked Woods.

She nodded. "In there. ME is here."

I walked in while Terry spoke with the officers. I addressed the ME. "Hey, Doc. What are your thoughts?"

"Heart attack seems like the most logical, but we'll know in a few weeks for sure."

"Where are you at with the Reynolds autopsy?" I asked, since they'd both died here, it could be connected.

"Not yet, but I'm expecting to have it to you this week."

"Great. I'll be interested if these two are at all related." Given that Joanna had mentioned Mr. Reynolds thought he'd been murdered, it only made sense to look at all angles.

I looked around. "Was he found here in bed?"

"Yes. He used oxygen, and it looks like it malfunctioned. Could've been tampered with, but it's an older model, so who knows?"

"I'll tag it for evidence. We'll have someone look at it."

"So, this is a much bigger police presence than you normally have for one of these. What's up?" Doc whispered to me.

"The caller said they suspect he was murdered."

"Ah, well, we'll find out for sure once we get the autopsy and get back to you."

I quickly gathered what I could before they took the body, then watched Dr. Starke finish getting the body prepped. With the help of his latest intern, they got it loaded and taken away.

With that gone, I looked for evidence of foul play on the bed. I would focus on anything in the room. I slipped on some latex gloves and got to work.

Nothing unusual on the bed. It looked as though the man had been sleeping peacefully, extremely peacefully. I said a little prayer for him. Though I wasn't a church-going person, I had faith.

I looked over the oxygen machine. I wasn't familiar enough with them to know what could be wrong. We had a whole department that would be able to examine it. But I did note it making an odd hissing sound. I switched it off and then signaled for the forensic team to tag it.

Terry joined me in the bedroom as I was going through the man's desk. I was looking for anything on the oxygen machine. Maintenance receipts or a user manual, anything that could give me information about how it worked and if there were any recent repairs.

"Finding anything good?" he asked.

"Not really." I thumbed through an old file folder. It was full of user manuals for various things, but no oxygen machine one.

"What exactly are you looking for?"

"Well, Doc said that it seemed the oxygen machine may have malfunctioned in some way. I was hoping to find a user manual or maybe something showing recent maintenance, but nothing."

"Um, I guess we'll have to see what Johnson says after he looks at it."

"Yeah, unfortunately, it doesn't look like there are many clues here. We'll see what the autopsy comes back with, I guess."

I also knew I'd have to get with Joanna again soon to see what her thoughts were on this, and if this victim had reached out to her yet. Then my brain tripped over itself. What was I saying? Did I actually believe this stuff now?

"What's that look on your face for?" Terry chuckled.

"I might be starting to believe Jo's voodoo nonsense."

He let out a booming laugh and slapped my back. "Welcome to the dark side, my friend."

We wrapped up our investigation, leaving the patrol officers to close up the scene and release it back to the staff. That's when I spied Kelli standing nearby with a few people comforting her, or perhaps they were all supporting each other.

"Kelli, hi," I said.

"Oh, Detectives, did you find out why our sweet Ruben died so suddenly?" She wiped at her eyes with one hand and held onto an older woman with the other.

"We don't have answers today, but we hope to know something more soon," I said.

"Are you doing okay?" Terry asked, placing a hand on her shoulder.

"Oh, I'll be okay. It's just Jack and now Ruben." She choked out. "They were some of my favorites here. Like a father or a favorite uncle." A few fresh tears slid down her face. One of the women hugged her. "Of course, Aggie, you're a favorite too. Oh, who am I kidding? I love everyone here."

They were all crying now.

I'd always been uncomfortable when women cried, or anyone for that matter. I shifted my weight from left to right and looked around. We needed to get to the station to file the reports and touch base with forensics to see what they collected. It would only be preliminary results, but it would get us started.

My phone chimed. It was Joanna.

Message from the dead

Ruben? I replied.

Yes

Can I stop by later?

Yes, please

We wished the ladies well and said goodbye. Back in the car, I relayed what Joanna's message said.

"Should we head over there now, or do you want to go alone?" Terry asked as he drove away from Birdsong.

"Probably best if we both go, yes? You think of questions that I don't always think of."

"And?"

"And I'm not ready to be alone again with her. There, happy?"

"Yes, and no." He said. "Obviously, I hate to see you unhappy, but I'm happy you admit, indirectly, that you miss her. You should talk to her about that soon."

I didn't reply, but I knew he was right. I'd proposed. I loved her and I couldn't just give up on that. She'd asked why I felt ready for marriage, and if I was serious, I needed to tell her my reasons. I just didn't know those reasons myself yet.

Chapter Thirteen

I was out walking Chewy with Oakley in the stroller, enjoying our Saturday morning. It had been rainy overnight. There were puddles on the sidewalk and in the street, and everything smelled clean and fresh. I loved it after a nice rain, even with the humidity. I took a deep, cleansing breath.

Oakley babbled and chatted away in the stroller while Chewy bounced along, smiling and tail wagging. He loved going for a walk.

"Hello? Hello? Are you Ms. Joanna the medium?" A man called out to me. My eyes focused on him. He looked like, yep, a spirit.

"Hi. Yes, that's me." I smiled but kept walking. He fell into step with me and walked along with us.

"Oh, thank goodness. I saw you yesterday at Birdsong and, well..." He gestured down. "I woke up, err, not woke up. Dead."

"I'm sorry. Do you know what happened?" I had a gut feeling he would say he was murdered.

"If I had to guess, I was, and I can't believe I'm going to say this, killed. Murdered."

Shocker. I tried to hide my lack of surprise.

"Oh, I'm sorry. Why do you think you were murdered, and by whom?" I tried to keep my voice even and calm.

"I'm not sure. Jack said you were helping him, so I thought maybe you could help me figure this out too."

I had a few suspects, but there were limited clues and even less to go on.

"Well, he gave me a few names. Do you have anyone who might not like you?"

He thought for a moment as we continued our walk. I was thankful for the rain last night as it meant the streets were deserted and I could talk to a ghost without people thinking I was the crazy person talking to myself. If anyone did happen to walk by, I'd just pretend to be talking to my daughter or the dog.

"Honestly, it could have been one of the crazy women. They were all looking for a man, and if we said we were still in love with our wives, even though they'd passed on, it made them even more interested in us."

"Seriously?"

"Yes. Saying no made them all act even crazier and lovesick." He paused. "You wouldn't believe the catfights and drama among the women."

"Do you know Odette? Uh, I didn't get her last name."

"Of course. Odette Tidwell. She's the worst at starting stuff. She hangs around with Robin Perkins and Alma Jean Gibson. Alma Jean isn't quite as dramatic as the rest, but Odette and Robin are thick as thieves and always in the middle of the drama."

I remembered the comment Odette had made yesterday after the reading. Could that be her secret? I wasn't going to accuse someone until I had more facts or reason to believe it was her, because honestly, her comment could have simply been about her husband seeing her date and what that might have meant.

"I'll look into it, and if you and Jack could get together on whether you think your deaths are related, that would be helpful."

"Alright. I'll talk to him. Well, I'll leave you to your precious daughter." He smiled at her. Of course, she couldn't see him. "I'll touch base with you soon."

He started to leave, but I realized I was missing one important detail.

"Wait, I forgot to ask, what's your name?"

"Oh, yes, of course. Ruben Harper."

"Nice to meet you, Mr. Harper."

"Please, call me Ruben."

I nodded, and we parted ways. I shot off a text to Clint. I was sure he knew about the death already, but just in case he didn't.

His reply was almost instant. He'd swing by later. My stomach flip-flopped. I knew I'd have to see him again at some point, but it didn't stop the nerves from kicking in.

I also realized I didn't ask Ruben if I would see him again and if so, when. He just said he'd see me soon.

"Darn it." I kicked at a small rock. Chewy looked at me, ears perked. "I'm sorry, boy. I'm okay."

We finished our walk and headed back to the house. I got Oakley out of the stroller, and she toddled over to one of the numerous balls that were strewn about and immediately started playing with Chewy. I watched them for a moment before heading to the kitchen to finish cleaning up from our breakfast.

After that, I started a load of laundry, then took out the trash. I then looked around for anything else to keep my mind off of my future visitor. My house was fairly clean, except for baby and dog toys, which were mostly balls.

As I watched them, I decided to try jumping into their game, but they were too preoccupied and basically ignored my attempts. Oakley even scolded me once for trying to throw the ball for them.

"No, Ma." She ran off after the dog, but neither let me get close enough to it after that.

"Well, excuse me." I chuckled, faking my annoyance. Honestly, I loved their friendship, and I knew he would protect her.

I watched them for a few minutes before grabbing my laptop so I could search for information on Ruben Harper. Who was he and what was his connection, if any, to Jack?

I should have asked him, but it had caught me a little off guard at the time. Were they simply neighbors or friends? As the search results started to populate, it became clear. They were not only friends, but they were the founding members of their technology company.

"I knew his name sounded familiar," I muttered.

I read a few articles, finding so many similarities between him and Jack. Both of their wives had passed, no children, and no other family.

"Hmm, that's strange."

Who would his estate go to? If these stories were correct, which I was sure they were accurate, he was quite wealthy. We were talking millions, just like Jack.

There was a knock at the door. Chewy barked in my direction and then did his spin and bark towards the door. Oakley was close behind him, yelling her version of door.

I scooped up the baby as I opened the door wide to find not only Clint, but Terry as well.

"Well, hello, detectives. Welcome." I gestured for them to come in.

Oakley reached out for Clint. "Da! Da!"

He smiled and took her from me.

"Can I get either of you something to drink?" I offered as they stepped inside.

"Water, please, Jo," Terry said with a smile.

"Same. Thanks," Clint mumbled as Chewy bounced along next to him.

They settled into the living room while I got them each a glass of water, then I joined them, setting the waters in front of each of them. I smiled as Oakley showed Clint and Terry all of her toys. Chewy was sitting at Clint's feet.

They loved him and had missed having him around. Truth be told, I had too. I looked up at him and smiled when our eyes met. He flashed a quick smile, but then looked back at the baby.

"You met with a new spirit?" Terry said.

"Yes, Ruben Harper. He said he was killed at Birdsong last night."

"Yeah, that's where we just came from," he confirmed, looking at Clint as he spoke. Clint simply nodded. "Did he give any idea of suspects?"

I tried not to laugh. "Not really, but he said he suspects all the women there."

"What?" Clint blurted with a short laugh.

"Yeah, Jack Reynolds gave me names of just women too."

"Did you find anything when you did your reading?" Clint asked.

I knew he still wasn't fully believing my powers, so his snarky tone wasn't lost on me. Hadn't I proven it time and time again?

"Not really. Though one of the ladies, Odette, did make a weird comment."

"What kind of comment?" Terry said, pen at the ready to make a note.

"Well, her deceased husband said he knows about her dating a lot of men. She didn't seem to like that he knew, and rhetorically asked me what he could have seen."

"Well, that could be something," Terry said. "We'll interview her."

"Did you get a last name?" Clint snipped.

It was a fair question, but I didn't understand his tone.

"Tidwell. Odette Tidwell." Confirmed by Ruben just this morning.

"And what were the other names? Do you know who she hangs out with?" Terry asked.

"Odette, Dawn Holmes, and Phyllis King are the names he gave me. Odette hangs out with Alma Jean Gibson, who is Laney's grandmother, and then Robin Perkins. Ruben told me Odette and Robin are in the middle of all the dramatic scenes at Birdsong. I've met them all, except Dawn."

"You met them when, recently?"

"Yes, Odette and Robin are friends with Laney's grandmother. I had lunch with her a week or so ago. Then I did a group reading there yesterday and did a reading for Phyllis. Ruben agreed that at least Odette would be one to look at and maybe her friend, Robin."

"Why do these men think it's these women? Was there a reason?" Terry asked.

"Love, lust, drama." I giggled, which won me a dirty look from Clint. I cleared my throat. "Apparently, they are desirable among the senior women and there was a lot of fighting over dating the few eligible men."

Terry laughed out loud. "Seriously?"

"Yes, the women told me as much over lunch. Odette thought she was dating Jack, but he said he was not. He was still in love with his wife who passed a few years ago."

"That's sweet. It's how I feel about Whitney," Terry smiled.

My eyes locked with Clint's for just a moment, then we both quickly looked away without commenting. I didn't know if Clint was thinking about us or him and Monica, but I knew for me, I immediately thought of my first husband.

Once upon a time, I'd felt that way for Ted, at least until his death when I learned of his secret life. He hadn't cheated on me at least, but he had been living a double life nonetheless. Still, when we first married, I could never have imagined myself with someone else. Could I now? Could it be Clint?

Then, because sometimes our hearts and brains could be fickle and maybe a bit cruel in taunting us, I had a flash of Eddie's face.

Just a crush, just a crush, I repeated to myself.

"Okay, well, we will look into these women and possibly others," Terry confirmed, and then he stood.

"Yeah, I would. It seems like there's a lot of fighting and things there."

They stood, and I scooped up Oakley so she didn't get in the way as I walked the two men out. Clint looked at me and he started to open his mouth, but then snapped it shut. I simply smiled as they walked out and down the driveway to their car.

"Da?" Oakley looked at me.

"He has to work, baby."

"Da!" She yelled with a lot of baby attitude in her tone.

He looked back at her and waved. "Bye, Oakie."

She giggled and seemed to be happy with that. She simply wanted a goodbye. When I shut the door, she toddled off with Chewy. I stood with my back to the door.

Was this going to be how all of our interactions would be from now on? Tension with snarky comments sprinkled in.

Chapter Fourteen

~ Joanna ~

It had been a week since my reading at Birdsong, and today I was returning for a tour with my parents. Since it was my day off, and my mother wouldn't forgive me if I didn't, I was bringing Oakley along with us.

Pulling up at their house, I realized the baby was asleep, so I dialed their phone to let them know I was here.

"Hello?" came my mom's voice over the line.

"Hi, Mom. I'm here."

"Why didn't you come to the door?"

"I didn't want to get Oakley out of the car. She just fell asleep."

"Oh, you have my grandbaby! We'll be right out." Before she hung up completely, I heard her yell to my dad.

I chuckled. My mom was a doting grandmother, and I loved that for both her and Oakley.

A moment later, my mom came jogging out, leaving my dad to juggle his crutches and lock the front door. She whipped the back door open and climbed in.

"Don't wake her up, please," I said, and then I got out to help my poor father into the car.

It had been about a month since his accident, and he was doing overall really well. He was in a walking boot now and didn't need the crutches quite as much. He would just need them today because we'd be walking quite a bit.

"Hi, Dad," I said as I opened the passenger seat for him.

"Hi, Jo." He got to the car and climbed in. "Thanks, sweetie."

My mom was desperately trying to wake up Oakley without waking her directly.

"Mom, I'm serious. Let her sleep or she'll be cranky during this tour."

"Fine." She pouted and stared out the window.

We drove over in near silence, just the soft music on the radio and the sound of the baby sleeping. I pulled down the long driveway that led to Birdsong's visitor parking.

"Oh, wow. Is this it?" My dad whistled.

"It is. Isn't it beautiful?"

"It looks like a resort with all these flowers and the gorgeous fountain." My mom pointed. "I love those turquoise blue tiles."

I parked in a handicap spot and put Dad's temporary tag in my windshield. He needed the extra space to get out of the car. I hopped out and ran around to his side of the car to help. Then I opened the trunk on my sedan to get Oakley's stroller.

My mom happily unbuckled her and lifted her from the seat. Oakley whined a little until she saw her gramma.

"Gam. Gam!"

"Hi, baby girl." She picked her up and held her while I ended up pushing an empty stroller. I should have probably left it behind, but I knew Mom would get tired from holding the baby at some point.

When we walked into the office, we were met by a smiling Velda. She looked happier than I'd seen her in the past. Her posture was relaxed, less tense.

"There's my favorite person." She flew around the reception desk to hug me. "I'm so happy to see you. Is she here?" Velda's eyes darted around hopefully.

I smiled at Hazel. "Yes, Hazel is here, and she says you look beautiful in the pink."

"That was always her favorite color." Velda smiled as she smoothed the front of her soft pink blouse.

My mother rolled her eyes and my dad just tried to be invisible. They still weren't completely comfortable seeing my powers in action, even if my dad supported me and loved that it got him free coffee at his favorite diner.

"So, hi, Mr. and Mrs. Webber. We're happy to have you here today," she said, turning her attention to the business at hand. "If you'll just give me your IDs, I will get y'all signed in." She took them. "Thank you."

She scanned them and then printed out a sticker badge, handing one to each of us when done.

"I have a wonderful tour guide set up for you. She isn't here yet. Oh wait, here she comes."

In walked Phyllis. Today she was rocking black skinny jeans with combat boots and an oversized Nirvana shirt with a chunky black cardigan.

She looked amazing. I could only hope to have this kind of vibe when I was her age or look this stunningly beautiful.

"Phyllis. These are the Webbers."

"Charlie and Babs." My dad extended his hand. "Nice to meet you."

My mom flashed a tight, fake smile and busied herself with Oakley.

"Nice to meet you both. Welcome." Phyllis smiled and then looked at me. "And I know you. Thank you for the sweet message last week." She leaned forward to hug me.

"Of course. Happy to do it." I beamed.

"Well, are y'all ready?"

"Yes," my dad and I said. My mom said nothing.

Was she going to be rude the whole time? I wanted to lecture her like a petulant child, but I was going to let it go for now.

"So here we are in the courtyard. The mailboxes are to the left there." She pointed to a doorway, and beyond it we could see the postal boxes. "In front of that is where Kelli posts our events. Kelli is the event coordinator. Out here in this garden, we do yoga, flexibility classes, or Tai Chi classes plus a few others. Great to stay active."

She showed us the swimming pool where a water aerobics class was happening. Several people waved to me. I smiled and waved back. I noticed a few looked at Phyllis and whispered amongst themselves.

I made a point to walk closer to Phyllis, not easy while dragging this empty stroller along with us, but I did the best I could. As I smiled at her, I ensured that the pool ladies were watching.

"I love your shirt. Nirvana is one of my favorites," I said.

"Oh, thanks. I love them too." She looked down at her shirt.

A few mouths in the pool fell open. Hopefully that caused a bit of gossip or maybe shut some of them up. We continued on our walk.

"And this is the arts and crafts room. Kelli is a doll about finding fun new crafts for us each week." We peeked in to find a craft class happening.

"Joanna!" The room cheered. Kelli jogged over and gave me a hug.

"Who do we have here?" She wagged a finger at Oakley, who

giggled and pointed to her. "Oh, she's friendly. Hi, Princess."

"That's my daughter, Oakley," I said with pride.

"She's precious." Then Kelli smiled at Mom and Dad. "Hi, I'm Kelli Wallace, Event and Activities Director here."

"I'm Charlie Webber and this is my wife, Babs."

"Oh, you're her parents." Kelli smiled at me. "I forgot she mentioned something about you moving here. What do you think?"

"It's nice," Dad smiled.

"What are y'all working on today?" I asked and was thankful that it wasn't as smelly as the first day I was here.

"We're doing painted pots. Aren't they cute?" Kelli said, picking one up to show us. "This is mine."

The names Jack, Ruben, and Carl were neatly painted onto her pot. I didn't know Carl, but Jack and Ruben I knew.

"Oh, is this for Jack Reynolds and Ruben Harper?"

She winced at the names. "It is. I miss them both terribly. And then Carl is a friend that passed about a year ago."

"I'm sorry to hear." I put my hand on her arm. I made a mental note of the name Carl. I'd do a search when I got home.

"Aw, thanks. You're so sweet." She looked around. "Are any of them here now?"

I noticed all the residents' eyes shifted to me as I looked around. Nobody stepped forward saying they were Carl, and I didn't see either Jack or Ruben.

"Sorry, not today."

"Well, maybe another day." She frowned. "I'll let you get back to your tour."

"Thanks," I said and waved around to the room of crafters.

When we stepped outside, Mom handed me the baby, so I strapped her into the stroller and finally didn't have to drag the empty thing around with us.

Phyllis then showed us the two cafeterias and the bistro. I'd already been to the bistro with Alma Jean and Laney, but my dad was especially interested in the food.

"So many choices!" He eyed the week's menu that was posted by each door of the different eateries.

"Too many choices," Mom pouted. "I love to cook."

"I love to cook too and prefer that, and let me tell you, the kitchens in the apartments here are wonderful," Phyllis said, smiling at my mom. "I'll show you our model units, and if we have time, we can swing by mine too so you can see how I have it set up, just to give you an idea. It's more personal than seeing the staged model, right?" She winked at Mom.

An expression flashed over Mom's face that told me she was warming up a bit to Phyllis. I knew she wanted to hate this place, but this really was going to be a good fit, if she would just accept it. Perhaps some of Phyllis' positive energy would transfer to Mom.

We arrived at the models. First, we looked at the one-bedroom. It was nice. Small and definitely not what my parents were used to. It would be an adjustment.

"There isn't room for my crafts, but I guess with the dedicated activities, that would be okay," Mom said. "I do like this kitchen okay, but there isn't enough counter space for me."

"The two-bedrooms, which is what I have, have better kitchens. You would have space for crafts or an office, plus extra closets and counters in there," Phyllis said. "There are more two-bedroom units here than the others, so chances are good you'll get one of those."

"That sounds good. Can we see that model?" Mom said cheerily.

"Of course."

Mom hooked her arm with Phyllis', and they smiled, walking arm in arm to the next unit. I'd never seen this side of my mother.

Walking into the larger one, I looked over to see my mom light up. This was going to sell it. The space was open and airy. The kitchen was bigger than the last with almost triple the counter space.

"Oh, wow, now this is what I'm talking about," Mom said, standing in the middle of the kitchen. She opened each and every cabinet and drawer. "I can really do some cooking in here."

"Yeah, I love it. There's enough counter space to roll out cookies or knead bread, which I love to do," Phyllis said.

"I love baking too," Mom smiled. "I used to always have something warm from the oven when the girls were little."

I sure did miss my mom's cookies. She always had a plate out when we'd get home from school.

After looking at this unit, Phyllis showed us her unit. It was decorated just as I would imagine. Clean modern furniture with straight lines and simple structure. Then she had her eclectic style reflected in the bright pops of color in the art, pillows, and throw blankets.

The frames were a mix of wood and metallic. The prints inside ranged from a silhouette of a cat, an elephant, to abstract florals, to a boho rainbow. Nothing matched, yet it all fit, just like Phyllis.

"Phyllis, your home is gorgeous," Mom said, taking it all in. This was not my mother's style, but I was so glad she wasn't being judgmental.

My mom was stuck in the 1980s with their white palm printed sofa and all the glass and rattan furniture with pastel rose and blue knick-knacks. I hoped that this potential move would have her upgrading her style a bit.

After taking in the kitchen and living room area, the two ladies toured the rest of it without Dad or me. We could hear them giggling from the other room.

"I guess we're moving," Dad said to me with a chuckle. "And at least she'll have a friend starting day one."

"It really looks that way."

Oakley was starting to get restless and getting whiny, but I didn't want to rush Mom. I took her out of the stroller to try comforting her. It made things worse because she just pushed against me to get down.

"I'm going to go outside with Oakley. I'll be close by."

My dad smiled and took a seat at Phyllis' kitchen table. It had been a lot of walking for him, so I saw him prop his leg before I shut the door.

I stepped outside and almost ran into Kelli, startling us both and causing me to nearly drop Oakley.

"Oh, I'm sorry," I said as I juggled a wiggly baby on my hip. Darn it, I should have put her back in the stroller.

"No, no. I'm sorry. I was right by the door."

"What were you doing?"

"Just walking by."

Oddly close to the door, which was strange behavior, but not the strangest. I had bigger issues though than what this stranger was doing. I needed to get Oakley somewhere she could run around.

"Um, okay." I looked at the baby. "Is there a good place that I can put her down so she can run a bit?"

"Yes, just over this way." She gestured for me to follow her.

We walked to the end of the units and there was an open area covered in grass with park benches around the edges. It had flowering trees and shrubbery trimmed flawlessly. It was open enough for Oakley to run around.

"This is our family garden. Created for families to let their little ones run around while still visiting with their family."

"It's perfect." I set my daughter down, and she looked around before darting towards the roses.

"P'ty!" She pointed, then sniffed in the general direction of the flower.

Kelli and I laughed, watching her as she tried to smell more of the flowers. She waddled around to a different patch of flowers, pointing and chattering about how pretty the flowers were and how good they smelled, or at least that seemed to be the gist of it.

"So, do you know yet if your parents will move here?" Kelli asked.

"I think so." I looked towards the general direction of Phyllis' apartment. "My mom and Phyllis seem to have hit it off."

"That might not be good for your mom," Kelli said.

"Why? Phyllis seems great." I had an idea of why but wanted to see what Kelli said.

"Well." She hesitated, looking around first, then lowered her voice. "Most of the other women around here don't like her. I don't blame them, really. She's sweet with many, but she always causes drama with a few of them, arguing and egging them on. Rumor has it, she also has been trying to steal their men."

"Oh."

That didn't seem to be what I observed, but I would at least hear her out. She knew her far better.

"Yeah, if your mom wants to fit in, she needs to cut any friendship with Phyllis."

"I'll let her know." Or maybe I would just let it play out how it did.

At that moment, my mom, dad, and Phyllis joined us. Phyllis was enjoying an e-cigarette that smelled like strawberries. Kelli looked at me and made a disgusted face. Perhaps she was as catty as the rest of the women here.

I actually liked Phyllis. She had vigor, a zest for life about her, and didn't care what others thought. She just did what seemed to make her happy.

"Well, what did you think?" Kelli asked. She was back to friendly, bubbly Kelli.

Fake! I thought but tried my best to keep a neutral face.

"We're thinking this is the place for us," Mom said as she smiled at Phyllis.

"That's wonderful," I said. I looked at Phyllis. "What are the next steps?"

"We'll go talk to Velda! I'm so excited for y'all to join us." She squeezed Mom around the shoulders.

They giggled like girls. It was sweet. Mom didn't have many friends, and the few she had were cranky like her. Phyllis was quite the opposite, and I hoped Mom stayed friends with her.

"I will let you get to that. I have to get to bingo," Kelli said, walking away and waving until she was out of sight.

Phyllis didn't look at Kelli, but I could see in her expression she didn't like Kelli any more than Kelli liked her. Phyllis caught my eye and winked as if trying to give me some kind of message. I didn't understand it, but I simply smiled in return and picked up the baby.

"Shall we head to the office?" she asked.

"Yes, let's go," I said, putting Oakley in the stroller.

We made our way to the office to sign some papers. I was so happy this was behind us, and they would be moving. It set my mind at ease.

No more falls from the roof for Dad.

Chapter Fifteen

Arriving at my office, I switched on the computer, hoping to find Jack Reynolds' autopsy results. I was expecting them any day now. If what Joanna said was right, that he was murdered, there should be a lead in the report.

"Nothing," I mumbled, at least not from Dr. Starke.

I clicked through the usual daily reports and news from our precinct. Our counterparts, Detectives Jackson and Simmons, had investigated a suicide last night.

As I scrolled through their report, a sadness washed over me. I hated hearing about someone taking their life. How lonely they must have felt in those final moments?

I got to the end, letting out a heavy sigh.

"Did you just read Jackson and Simmons' report?" Terry said at my door.

"I did. Star quarterback, full scholarship to his top choice college."

"Never know what's going through someone's mind or life. Very sad." He plopped in my guest chair. "Nothing from Starke yet."

"Yeah, saw that." I frowned, then looked up at my computer screen again, just in case it had popped up in the last few seconds.

"I thought it would be today."

"Me too," I said as I clicked refresh. Still nothing new popped up.

There was a knock at my door. Officer Woods stuck her head in.

"They need you both at a scene on Marshall near Cooper's Drug Store."

"Sure," Terry said, standing. "What's going on?"

"Found a body near the dumpster."

"Alright. Can you let them know we're on our way?" Terry said as he stepped out and grabbed his keys. I grabbed my cell phone and followed him out.

"At least this will be a distraction," I mumbled as we drove to the scene.

"Yeah, I wasn't going to get much done waiting on the

report." Terry said as he changed lanes. "Any word from Jo about this case?"

"A little. She said Mr. Reynolds visited her shortly after saying he was murdered, so there's that. She claims to not have done much digging yet, but you know her. She can't help herself."

"Well, I would hope that having Oakley and after a few incidents, she would learn her lesson," Terry said.

I thought about that. On the Senator's case, she'd really tried to stay out of trouble. It just happened that Vera figured out she knew more than she'd let on. I couldn't fault Joanna completely in that.

"She has gotten better at staying out of trouble. I think her curiosity can be useful if used in the right way, like asking the right questions or knowing which threads to pull."

"Wow." He snickered. "A bit of a change of heart towards her?"

"I may be hurt, but I can see the good in her." I scowled. "I wanted to marry her after all."

Our conversation ended there as we pulled up at the scene. The patrol officers had the scene secured and media was getting set up beyond the barrier.

I saw a body covered and just out of sight of public view. Dr. Starke's second in command was here to certify the body and pick it up. Hopefully the doc was back at the office working on the report to us, or at least signing off on it to be sent to us.

We headed over to touch base with the officer in charge, then we took our usual roles with Terry speaking to the media and I examined the scene.

Several hours later, we headed to Quench for some lunch. A barbecue bacon burger was a definite necessity after a long morning.

"Hey, Terry and Clint!" Angel greeted when we walked in. "Let's see. I have a spot in Chris' section. Right this way."

We followed her to the booth.

"Thanks, Angel." I smiled at her.

She beamed back, squeezing my shoulder. "Anything for my favorite customer." She turned, leaving us there. I studied the menu, knowing full well I was going to order the same thing I always got.

"She likes you," Terry said, over his menu.

"Who?"

"The hostess."

"Angel? Nah, she's just doing her job."

"Sure. That's it." He chuckled.

I stared at him. Could she? No way. Even if she did, she was too young for me and not my type. My type was a brunette with stunning brown eyes and just enough curves that it caused my blood pressure to rise and my palms to get sweaty. I shook off that thought because she was out of reach at the moment.

"Hey, gentlemen." Chris came to our table. "The usual for you, Clint?"

"You know what, no. I'm going to try something new." I ran my eyes quickly over the menu and tried to avoid Terry's inquisitive smirk. "Mushroom Swiss burger and a Coke."

"Well, alright. I love it." Chris chuckled. "And you, Terry?"

"I'm going with Clint's usual. Barbecue bacon with extra grilled onions and an iced tea."

"Very good. I'll get this in and then bring your drinks in a sec."

I watched Chris hustle away and tried not to look at my partner. I knew he was going to rib me for my break in character. He did not disappoint.

"Mr. Hartley, why the sudden change?" He jabbed.

"I don't know. Just felt like something different."

"We've known each other for, what? Seven, eight years. You are nothing if not predictable."

"People change." I shrugged.

"Enough to ask out someone new and outside your norm? Perhaps on our way out today?"

I shifted uncomfortably under his intense stare and line of questioning. No, I wouldn't ask out Angel on our way out. It took me a year or more before I went on a first date after Monica, and that one was just to appease my mother.

I couldn't even picture myself with anyone else other than Joanna at this point.

"Maybe so."

He laughed then, thankfully, changed the subject to work topics. I was far more comfortable in this space.

Chris dropped our food while we were discussing the department's recent memo about the change to vacation. They'd given us all a few extra days, trying to encourage people to take them. It was a problem at our station that I heard wasn't common.

"I have enough trouble finding time for vacation. Between our schedule and Whitney's, we can't seem to match up."

"I love our job. When I have taken off, I'm just thinking about work."

As if on cue, our phones chimed that we had a message.

"Dr. Starke. He says he sent over the report."

I looked around for Chris, signaling for the check when I had his attention. I shoved the rest of my burger in my mouth as we waited, and then we both nearly sprinted out once the bill was settled.

We had a roughly twenty-minute drive back to the station and my body hummed with adrenaline. We would have an answer to whether this was murder or simply age-related soon.

"Should you message Jo to give her a heads-up?" Terry asked.

"Why?"

"She's part of this investigation, so I thought she might want to know, especially if she can tell the victim and give him peace of mind."

Did he seriously just say that? Peace of mind for the victim. I mean, I knew that was supposed to be Joanna's deal, but we usually worked with the survivors, the family and friends left behind. I knew I'd opened my mind about her powers, but I wasn't a complete believer yet.

"Not until I know what it says."

We pulled into the station parking lot and made our way inside.

"Did y'all hear the results of your case are in?" Jackson asked as we passed her in the hallway.

"Did you see them?" I asked.

"No, they kept them tight. I'm assuming that means your medium friend is right. Murder." She said with a nod, then continued her path towards her own office.

We both rushed into my office as I pulled up the report. We skimmed it together.

"Nicotine poisoning," I mumbled.

"Unless he did this to himself, he was murdered."

"I don't remember us finding any nicotine products in his apartment."

"Yeah, no forms of it at all."

We'd recently moved to more electronic forms of reporting, so I pulled them up on my computer to double check. We read it together twice.

"Nope. Nothing," I confirmed.

The nicotine concentrations in his blood, urine, and contents of his stomach and small intestine were six point three micrograms, one point five micrograms, thirty micrograms, and seventy-one micrograms. Not normal at all, especially considering we didn't find anything in his belongings pointing to him being a smoker or using these products at all. There also wasn't a suicide note or indication that he'd taken his life.

Joanna was right. Another victim that came to her with a murder.

"Damn," I mumbled.

"You're thinking about how Joanna is right again, aren't you?" Terry chuckled.

"No." Yes, but I wasn't going to tell him.

"I believe you." He smirked.

"Did y'all see the report?" The chief's voice sounded at the door.

"We just finished going over it," Terry straightened.

"You need to get back over there to Birdsong and go through his apartment again. We still have it sealed." He pointed at us. "Then start interviewing people again."

He turned to leave, but spun around, adding, "Oh, and find out what that medium knows."

I slowly nodded. I knew when these results came out that I'd have to talk to her again, especially with it coming back as murder, but I wasn't excited to see her again.

That was a lie. I couldn't wait to see her and hoped that she would be willing to talk about us. Not just the case.

"I'll talk to her today."

But first, we would head to Birdsong to go through Jack Reynolds' things again. There had to be something we'd missed, and now that we knew what we were looking for, it would be easier.

We arrived at Birdsong, got checked in with Velda, then made our way to the apartment. The door was still sealed from when our team closed it out. We hadn't been back since.

Entering, I was hit with the faint smell of Old Spice and the stale scent of an unused space. His place was neat with minimal decorations.

A sailboat painting over the brown sofa, a worn-out recliner with an end table between them. There was a tall lamp in the corner with a simple beige shade. No television, no computer. He had a wall of books between his bedroom and living room.

We spent the next two hours combing through every inch of his apartment. Starting with his books. We pulled each one out to see if there was a hidden note or compartment that would give us clues to the origin of the nicotine.

Next, we went through his dresser drawers and closet.

"I got nothing. Not even a piece of lint," Terry said after going through Mr. Reynolds' clothes.

"I guess we have to rule out a suicide," I commented.

"Yep. So now we move on to the murder investigation part. Who wanted him dead?"

"Joanna might have an idea. She was supposed to have that event here a few weeks ago, and said she was going to check out some leads."

"Alright. Should we go talk to her?"

"Okay. I'll message her."

Chapter Sixteen

"Well, that's the end of our time. Do you have any final words?" I said to my current clients, the Rossi family.

"Just that I will be here for her and the children as long as I can," Mr. Tony Rossi said. I translated for him.

"I will miss you forever, Tony." Mrs. Sheryl Rossi said as she rocked the baby in her lap. "I'll make sure that the children don't forget you, and especially that little Stewie here knows about you."

I handed her a tissue. She smiled as she wiped a tear and then stood, putting the baby into his car seat and gathering the toddler's toys. The oldest was about five and she started to whine a bit.

"Sunny, that's enough. It's time for us to go," Sheryl said firmly. "Thank Ms. Joanna for her time."

"Thank you, Ms. Joanna," Sunny said.

"You're welcome."

"Tank you," the middle son, Gavin, said.

"Aw, and you are welcome too." I smiled at him and then at Sheryl. "Your children are so well-behaved."

"Thank you. They've been through a lot. Spent a lot of time sitting by their father's bedside." Her voice caught as she spoke. "I really appreciate you doing this. It has given me some peace."

"It's my pleasure."

We walked out to the reception area, and I was startled to see both Clint and Terry sitting there. I tried to keep my posture and expression professional so that I didn't alert my client to any tension.

"Well, Mrs. Rossi, again, it was my pleasure." I turned towards the detectives. "Gentlemen, would you follow me?"

They stood and followed me as I held the door open between the reception and the back offices. I held a tight smile as Clint passed me. I wanted so badly to reach out and touch him, but of course, I didn't.

"How's Oakley doing?" Terry asked as we walked towards my office. "I bet she's getting big."

"Oh, she is. I can barely keep up with her." I laughed.

"Aw, they grow so quickly."

"Yes, they do. Speaking of, how's your crew doing?"

"Keeping us running. They all have their activities and interests. Whitney's amazing at keeping us all going in the right direction."

"I hope to be like her when I grow up, you know, as a mom."

I'd only met her once, but she was a wonderful lady. She loved her family and seemed to have it all together.

Terry gave a slight chuckle at my joke. I caught Clint's eye roll.

We reached the door of my office. I wanted to stall a bit further.

"Would either of you like coffee or water?"

"None for me, thanks," Terry smiled.

"No. Thank you," Clint mumbled.

"Well, if you would allow me a moment to get some water for myself?"

They nodded, so I gestured for them to head into my office while I headed to the break room to grab myself a drink and steady my nerves.

"Why does he unnerve me like this?" I muttered as I slowly walked away.

But honestly, was it him or the potential news he brought? We were in the process of moving my parents to Birdsong, and if someone was murdering people there, I was putting my parents in harm's way.

Then again, most of the murders I'd investigated turned out to be people known to the victim. I knew that wasn't always the case, but Cate knew her victims, Ted's parents obviously knew him. Then there was Vera and Hedy. Donovan wanted to get to me, but he didn't know his victims, so that was the only wrinkle in that theory.

Still, I thought they should be relatively safe there, much safer than Dad falling from the roof again.

I sighed and headed back.

"Sorry to keep you waiting. It's been a full day," I said, taking a seat at my desk.

Since I'd been in readings for the past two hours, I fought the urge to grab my cell phone to do a quick check for messages. Janie, my sitter, knew to call Tessa if there was ever an emergency, so I knew my daughter was fine. It was mostly habit and a stalling technique.

"So, what brings you by today?"

"We got the autopsy results for Mr. Jack Reynolds," Clint said flatly.

My hands started shaking, so I pressed them to my thighs to steady myself. "And?"

"It shows fatal levels of nicotine in his body."

"Murder then?"

"We think so," Terry said.

"We just wanted to reconfirm the names and find out if you'd learned anything new," Clint added.

"I haven't found out anything new since I told you about Odette's comment. Oh, that is Odette Tidwell."

Terry made a note.

"Remember she made a comment about what her husband might have seen her do," I added. "The other names are Phyllis King and Dawn Holmes. Honestly, Dawn seems like a dead end. I think he was just giving me names. Odette also hangs out with Robin Perkins. Ruben said that the two of them were always together and in the middle of all the drama."

"Do you happen to know if any of them use nicotine products? Or anyone else there that sticks out?" Clint asked.

"Both Phyllis and Odette do. And there are a number of other residents that do as well. A few smoke traditional cigarettes, but I noticed a lot of those e-cigarettes."

"Okay. I guess we have our work cut out for us then," Terry said, looking over at Clint. "I didn't think it was going to be obvious, but worth a shot."

"I actually hadn't had a lot of contact with Jack. He comes, demands answers, and then disappears. Like I mentioned before, he seems to believe everyone loves him and he thought of himself as a hunk among the ladies." I laughed. "I honestly think he liked the attention."

Terry chuckled.

Clint gave us both a death stare. This was the Clint I remembered from my first dealings with him. Stoic, icy with a slight arrogant vibe about him, like he knew best and everyone was just wasting his time.

"Well, be that as it may, he was murdered, and we need to

get to the bottom of this. We're still waiting on Ruben Harper's autopsy, but if it shows nicotine, we have a serial killer at Birdsong," Clint said.

"I can try to find him. Speak to some of the other spirits that hang about." The ones in my office all looked towards me, then nodded, leaving through the walls and unopened windows. "They're on it."

Both detectives looked around my office with wide eyes.

"Um, well, good." Terry cleared his throat. "Is there anything else you can think of that could help us?"

"I really can't think of anything right now."

"Okay. Well, we'll get out of your hair. We have a lot of people to look into now, so thanks for those names," Terry said with a smile.

Clint simply nodded as they walked out. I didn't bother to walk them to reception like I normally would, but as they got to my doorway, Eddie walked in.

"Oh, hey, detectives!" He reached out to shake their hands.

"Hey, Eddie. How's it going?" Terry said.

"Good, good." He nodded at Clint, who returned the gesture. "Well, I have some Hank business to discuss with Ms. Joanna. If you'll excuse me."

He stepped in and shut the door between us and the detectives. I could see Clint's nostrils flare through the window. Eddie turned towards me with a huge grin.

"I love messin' with him."

"That's a bit mean." I giggled.

"You love it, and you know it."

"No, not really. I don't have any reason to be intentionally cruel to him."

Though if he was a little jealous, so be it. Maybe it would force him into actually having a meaningful conversation with me.

"Well, if you were my girl, I wouldn't have given up so easily. No is just a word." He winked.

A tingle ran along my spine. Eddie was an attractive man, and if the timing was better, I would take him up on that wink.

"So, what's this about Hank business?"

"Oh, yeah." He grinned. "He wants to see you."

"He does?"

"Yes, and I already asked Tessa. You're done for the day, so can I give you a lift?"

"I have my car."

"I can bring you back to pick it up later," he said. "Maybe we can grab some dinner after you meet with Hank. Just as friends, of course."

I looked at him. He was all muscle and dimples. I'd known him for over a year now and I trusted him with my life. If he said just as friends, he meant it.

"Alright. Let me just finish up here. Just a few minutes."

"Great." He plopped himself down in one of my guest chairs.

I hadn't expected him to hang out here. I simply smiled and busied myself with answering a couple of emails, sending Tessa a quick message before finally shutting down.

"Ready," I said, grabbing my purse and cell phone.

He stood and gestured for me to go ahead of him. We smiled at Tessa as we walked past her. He then opened his truck, offering his hand to help me up into it. He had one of those jacked-up trucks that I could never get into without getting a running start then jumping in. I'd never really done that, though the thought had crossed my mind.

"Thanks." I tried to climb up gracefully. I slipped, and he grabbed my waist, setting me into the truck. I felt silly and a bit turned on by that. Darn it, I wanted to keep with the spirit of just friends, but that was a sexy move. "Whoops. Thanks again."

"No problem." He grinned as he shut the door, then jogged around to the driver's side.

We didn't talk much for a couple of blocks, but then we both tried to speak at the same time.

"You go ahead." Again, we said at the same time. We laughed.

I pointed at him. "You first."

"I was just going to ask about your parents. I know you were looking at getting them into Birdsong."

"Oh, yes." I didn't remember telling him that, but I must have at some point. "They move in this Friday, actually."

I'd taken the day off, as had Stan. Janie was going to keep Harris, Dylan, and Oakley. Plus, we had movers and packers coming in. This was an all-hands-on-deck venture.

Over the past few weeks, Audrey and I had been assisting them pare down. They'd lived in that house for over thirty years. Moving in when Audrey was still a baby, and I wasn't yet a thought.

It was going to be strange not going to my childhood home to visit them once they did move, but it was long overdue.

"Do you need any help? We've got lots of muscle and extra hands," he offered.

"Thanks. We hired a moving company. They'll have people to pack and then load up the truck. The works."

"That's gotta be expensive. Let us do it."

"I'll think about it."

"Well, think fast. Friday is in only three days," he quipped.

I simply smiled and turned to look out the window as I could feel my face warm.

We pulled into Leo's. I hadn't been here in about a month or two and hadn't spoken with Hank since the day with his mother when she admitted to killing his father.

I didn't know how Hank was feeling or what he wanted to speak to me about, but I knew this was likely going to be the first time he didn't ask me about his mother.

Stepping in, I was greeted with loud, boisterous voices calling out hello. Al, Hank's normally stoic right-hand man, grabbed me in a huge bear hug. I hadn't seen him in a few weeks either. Not since I'd had a tea party with his mother and sisters. I loved them.

He released me and Darius, the bartender, handed me a vodka cranberry before my eyes could even adjust to the dimly lit bar. Al then escorted me to Hank's table.

"Hello, Ms. Joanna," Hank greeted as his date excused herself. He almost always had a woman with him and never allowed them to stay when he talked business. "Thank you for coming. How are you doing?"

"I'm well. How are you?" I reached for his hand, and he allowed me to take it. "We haven't spoken since..."

I let my voice trail. I didn't need to say more. He knew when we'd spoken last, just as I did.

"I'm doing okay. Trying to forgive her and come to terms with things, especially when it comes to my father."

"Wow, that's progress. You weren't calling him that last time we spoke."

He chuckled. "It took some time, but I realized family has a huge impact on decisions and influencing how we react. He had a massive responsibility to run the family estate. He made the best decision he could at the time."

I nodded and released his hand. "Well, that's great. I think he definitely had regrets about it."

"Yeah." He smiled. "But that's not why I called you here. Your parents are moving to Birdsong soon, yes?"

"Um, yes. How did you know?" I knew for a fact I hadn't told Hank. Had Eddie told him?

"I have my sources. Anyway, I've heard that they've had a bit of trouble over there and I wanted to see if you knew about it."

"The two deaths?"

"Yes. Murdered is what I've heard."

"How? Where?" I was nearly speechless. How did he know this?

"Sources," he said apathetically. "We do the security there and hear a lot of things."

"Ah, now that makes sense. I didn't realize you did the security. It makes me feel better about my parents moving in."

"With them moving there, I was wondering if you were involved in the investigation. Have the gentlemen come to see you?"

"They have. Jack Reynolds gave me a few names, and Ruben Harper confirmed those were some to look at."

"Okay, good. And the detectives, they're working on it?"

"Yes, I just was meeting with them, actually. They got the autopsy back on Jack." I paused, not sure if I was allowed to share, but I knew Hank could and would find out whether it was from me or not. "Nicotine poisoning."

"Interesting. So, the leads you have, any that stand out?"

"Honestly, not yet."

"Well, let me know if you need assistance. I have guys that can do everything."

I knew that was true from our past work together.

"Thank you."

"Now for your parents' move, when can I have my crew over there to get everything packed and loaded?"

"Um." I looked up at Al. He raised an eyebrow but didn't say a word. "Eddie mentioned, but we have a company hired. They'll do all the packing and moving for us. I can't ask you to help with that."

"Nonsense." He snapped his fingers and people came from all around us. He started barking orders and looking at me for answers like date and time, but never asked for their address. I supposed he knew that. "Alright. Done."

"Thank you. I do appreciate you."

"I appreciate you too, Ms. Joanna. You've become a good friend." He waved his hand to his date. "Now if you'll excuse me, I'm going to get back to my date. Um, honey, what was your name again?"

"Ginger." She giggled as she slid in next to him and snuggled right up against him.

"Ah, yes. Sorry, at my age..." I couldn't hear the rest of his conversation as I'd walked away from him.

Al walked me to the door where Eddie was waiting.

"Ready for dinner?" he asked.

Al's head snapped to look at me. I just gave him a smile and then nodded to Eddie. I had no plans to make a big deal out of this. It was dinner with a friend. Nothing more.

Chapter Seventeen

~ Joanna ~

"Why is it the day before a day off feels like it takes forever?" I said, leaning on the reception desk.

"I don't know. But thanks for the extra day off this week, boss," Micah said.

"Yes, looking forward to a day off," Tessa said.

We were waiting on the last appointment for the day and then we would all start our weekend. Of course, mine was going to be taken up with getting Mom and Dad moved and their old house cleaned up.

"Y'all act like I work you to death. And might I remind you both, we get a lot of Fridays off already." I laughed. Heck, Micah wasn't even exactly my assistant. He just preferred that title better than partner.

"True, but weekends are the best," Tessa sighed and did a half spin in her chair.

"It gives me an extra day for wedding planning," Micah added.

"Yeah? How's that going?" I asked.

"Well, we found this wedding resort down in Key West. We're doing a little more research, but we're leaning towards this might be the way to go."

"What? Wow! Tell us about it."

"It's an all-inclusive island resort. There are two wedding parties each week, but the way they have it laid out and structured, it feels like you're on your own private island. Though there are some common activities, if we choose." Micah continued to tell us various details. His excitement was apparent in his giddy tone.

"It sounds amazing, but I have to ask, will it just be you guys and your families going?"

"Of course, families and friends are going! We still want you both. Oakley must be our flower girl. She must."

"Okay, yes, I'm in for sure." I leaned forward, hugging him.

"Me too! I have to be there for my best buddy," Tessa said, offering her fist for a bump.

"Wonderful. I hadn't even considered a destination wedding until this popped up," he said.

"Well, it sounds perfect. An island in the Keys? Yes, please," I said.

After a bit more chatting, our next client showed up. I greeted them with a smile, then led them back to start our session. An hour later and the workday was over.

I was shutting down my computer when two figures came through the wall.

"Jack, Ruben. Hello," I said, greeting them.

"Hello, dear," Jack said first.

"We heard you wanted to speak to us."

"I do. Yes." I stopped myself from asking them to have a seat. They couldn't exactly do that. "Well, we got back your autopsy results, Jack, and it shows high levels of nicotine."

"Nicotine! I'm not a smoker. At least not since I was a teen. I quit when I married and had our first child."

"It's not like that. They think liquid nicotine was added to your food or a drink. Poisoned."

"So, it was murder! I was right." He looked at Ruben. "I wonder if yours will show the same."

"I hope so. It would be nice to know how all this happened."

"Any new ideas on suspects? Have you been able to do any of your own investigating?"

It had been my experience that many of these ghosts got a bit lazy. They wanted me to do most of the work, but these two were go-getters, so I was hopeful.

"Nah, mostly we've just been visiting with other spirits and enjoying our afterlife."

"Seriously? I thought you wanted to figure out who killed you."

"Then what's your job?" Jack asked.

Was he serious? His stony expression said he was.

"I'm a medium. That's my job. I'm not a private investigator or a detective or even a medical examiner who understands all this fully. I connect dead people to their living loved ones." I didn't mention my new side gig with the police.

"Then what about the Landon boy?" Ruben asked.

"And that serial killer business?" Jack asked.

"Dumb luck and being overly curious."

"Then get some of that curiosity for our case. Ask people. Get out there," Jack said, more like a pep talk than an order, and I almost fell for it.

"I'm trying, but I need more to go on than everyone loved us and the women are jealous. It just doesn't seem realistic."

Also, it seemed a bit arrogant of them and a touch misogynistic, maybe. In spite of that, I'd witnessed a bit of that drama myself though, so who knew?

"I gave you the names I thought it could be. Odette, Robin, Dawn, and Phyllis. Those ladies were always fighting, and it seemed to be around us," Jack said, looking at Ruben for confirmation.

"Yeah, they were always arguing. It didn't even always have anything to do with us."

"So, it was about the two of you or it wasn't?"

"Both," Jack said.

"Both? Both of you or both about you and not?" This conversation got more and more confusing.

"Yes. Both about us and not," Jack nodded.

"And yes, it was fighting about both of us," Ruben added.

"Okay." That was as clear as mud.

"So, are you good? You can do your job now?" Jack asked.

I bit my tongue, because outside of doing some consulting for the police department, this was not my job. I also wanted to say no, they hadn't given me enough.

"Just one more question. I know you both worked at ReynHarp Software and Technology, Inc. Could there have been someone from there or a rival, perhaps?" I forced a smile.

They looked at each other.

"What about Dave?" Jack said.

"Nah, he's retired now, and he made a pretty penny taking that package."

"Right, right."

"What about Sam?" Ruben asked. "He hated us. Said he would ruin us if it was the last thing he did."

"Dead."

"Oh, that's right. Last year from a heart attack."

I watched them bat names back and forth for another minute or so. Everything they were saying made sense given their former role in life as founding members of ReynHarp Software and Technology, Inc., but unfortunately, it didn't seem to amount to anything.

"Well, I think that's everyone," Jack said, then turned to me. "I think it's on you to interview and investigate the ladies we mentioned. It happened at Birdsong, so it's someone there."

I sighed with the realization that they were right. The killer was at Birdsong. The place I'd deemed safe enough for my parents was now starting to look a bit scary and unsafe. It had been wishful thinking on my part that the killer would be someone else, somewhere else.

"Okay. I'll look at them closer."

"Good, good. Now we'll get back to our new life or whatever. We'll check with you in, say, a week," Jack said.

They didn't wait for my reply before they were gone.

I cursed under my breath. I had a big day tomorrow and didn't need another distraction. But I knew I would work on this. I just needed to get my parents moved and settled first.

I grabbed my stuff to head out for the day, but then thought I should probably reach out to Clint. I knew he and Terry were going to interview the women, though I didn't know if they had yet.

I shot off a quick text:

Talked to Jack and Ruben. Call if you get time.

With that done, I headed out. I didn't know when I would hear from Clint, but I needed to get Oakley and then head over to my parents.

We were having one final family dinner before the move tomorrow. Audrey was providing the food, and I had all the paper products so we wouldn't have dishes. We'd already had half of them packed up, but Hank said his team would handle the rest.

My phone rang as I got on the road. I hit the button for Bluetooth, putting the call through my car speakers.

"Hello."

"Hey, Jo." Goosebumps ran across my arms hearing his deep, smooth voice.

"Hey, Clint. Thanks for calling me so quickly."

"You said you spoke with our victims, so I knew it was important."

As illogical as it was, disappointment washed over me. I knew

I'd asked him to call, but it still hurt a little to hear him say that was the only reason he called.

"Yes, they didn't come up with any new names. They're sticking with the ones I gave you and Terry before."

"Alright."

"Have you gotten to interview them yet?"

"Not yet. We're working on search warrants so we can search apartments along with interviews. Probably tomorrow."

"By the way, my parents move in there tomorrow. Just in case we bump into each other." My chest tightened at the thought of possibly seeing him.

"Oh. Well, good luck. Maybe we'll see you tomorrow." Did his voice crack or was I reading my emotions into his reaction? "Let me know if you need anything."

"Thanks. I will."

There was a silence through the phone.

"Can we get coffee early next week?"

"Yes, I'd like that."

"Okay, I'll touch base with you then. Bye."

The call ended. A lump formed in my throat. I missed him so much. Even though I knew I was the one to suggest the break, I still loved him.

Not wanting to think about it, I turned the radio up a bit and continued on my way to pick up Oakley and Chewy.

Janie had everything ready when I arrived home.

"Thanks, Janie. You're an angel for having everything ready." I grabbed the diaper bag she'd packed up.

"Of course. Happy to help my favorite people." She kissed Oakley on the head, then we all walked out.

I waved to Janie as she drove away and then got the baby and dog into the car.

"Alright, let's go to Grandma and Grandpa's house for the last time."

She cheered. I smiled, but knowing this was the last time I'd be there had a mix of emotions washing through me.

We drove over, singing along with Oakley's kid music that she loved so much, and I kept an eye on our surroundings just in case we were being followed. It felt silly at this point because nothing had happened during this investigation, not like with others.

We pulled up to see that Audrey and family were already here, as was our Aunt Susie. It would be so nice to spend time with family.

"Knock. We're here," I announced, stepping in. I let go of Chewy's leash and set Oakley down.

"Gam?" She called out.

"Oh, there's my baby." Mom rushed in, scooping her up.

Aunt Susie came in, hugging me. "It's good to see you again."

"Yes, we're so glad you've been able to visit us."

"Me too. Work has been crazy, and it's been difficult to get away." She looked around. "It's been a while. Is Mark here?"

Mark was her high school boyfriend. She'd never completely let him go.

I smiled at him. "He is. He loves your haircut like this."

She touched the pixie cut. "Really? I wasn't sure about it."

"He says it brings out your eyes. He misses you."

"I miss him too. I've missed you having your powers too. So glad they're back and so strong again."

She touched my arm, then we joined the rest of the family in the kitchen and attached eating area.

It was wonderful to spend this one last time in my family home with some of my favorite people. I smiled as I walked out for one of the last times.

Tomorrow we would do our final walk out, but tonight the moment was full of love and family. I wanted to hold that feeling for just a moment more. I wept quietly as I drove away.

Chapter Eighteen

It was finally moving day for Mom and Dad. I'd received the cancellation from the moving company I'd hired, and now I was waiting on Hank's team to arrive. As I stood looking out the front window, I didn't know who or what to expect from this.

Would it be Eddie, Darius, T, and all the muscle who hung out playing pool and drinking beer at Leo's?

I laughed at the thought of Percy packing my parents' china cabinet or Eddie handling their clothing. Not that they couldn't do it, but they had much different day jobs and pasts that it made me chuckle.

"What's so funny?" Audrey said, coming up behind me.

"Just wondering what to expect from our new moving crew."

"Yeah, Hank employs quite an eclectic team."

"Can you imagine Percy or Al packing up Mom's delicate china and glassware?" I raised my arms up to about Al's height and then out for his giant shoulders.

He was a massive guy who'd carried me out of the woods in Appleton when I'd been abducted by the Playhouse Killer. I wasn't exactly petite. He always looked serious and ready to jump into action at the slightest move.

"He doesn't seem like the type to shy away from a job," she laughed.

"No, he definitely is not. He's a jack of all trades."

At that moment, two white box trucks with no logo and no name pulled up along with three dark SUVs. Men and women poured out of all of them. I recognized some faces, but others I didn't know.

I opened the door. Eddie was the first there, grabbing me into a bear hug.

"Hey, Jo!" Eddie said as he put me down.

Darius grabbed me next and then passed me off to Al. Then I noticed Hank walked up the sidewalk.

"Good morning, Joanna," he said as he got close, then hugged me too. "We're here to help."

"Great. I'm so glad to see everyone."

I turned to point them in the starting direction when I noticed my family behind me staring wide-eyed with their mouths practically hanging open. I gave them a get it together look and then turned back towards our movers.

What did they think these mobsters were going to do? Okay, maybe I knew what they thought, but they'd met many of them before. Did they feel like I was inviting vampires into the house?

"Please come in. Everything in the house goes. Ignore anything in the garage. That's going to be picked up by the women's shelter later."

"Great," Al said and then turned to start giving orders.

Everyone filed in, assessed the needs and level of effort, before heading to one of the trucks to grab moving boxes, tape, and other supplies. They trooped back into the house and dispersed throughout.

They were like a well-oiled machine, and I felt in the way, but Audrey and I jumped in where needed and answered questions.

We made Mom and Dad go ahead to Birdsong. They were going to have lunch with Phyllis, then the ladies were going to arts and crafts with Kelli while Dad was going to play poker with some guys he'd met. I was so glad that they were already making friends and enjoying activities there.

"So, how are you doin'?" Eddie said when we were alone.

We were taking the packed boxes from my parents' room to the truck.

"I'm good, but I'll be better when this is behind us," I said as I handed him a box.

"I bet." He stood there looking at me but didn't move to add it to the dolly. I felt my face warm as he finally said, "I had a nice time with you the other day."

"Oh, yeah, I did too." I smiled and grabbed the next box. I stacked it on the dolly instead of handing it to him.

He chuckled softly as he set his box on top of the one I'd just set down. He then tipped it up and rolled it out. Note to self: do not be alone with Eddie or sort through my feelings on him before letting it happen again.

A few hours later, my childhood home was empty of all the familiar furnishings. The only thing remaining was the decades-old wallpaper and carpet that should have been replaced many, many years ago. The new owners had a plan to replace it all.

Hank and the team headed over to Birdsong, while Audrey and I stayed behind for a final goodbye. We stood there, arms around each other, as we took it all in.

"So many memories," she whispered.

"So many," I repeated.

Hand in hand, we walked through each room. We didn't speak, just silently moved through our memories. I touched the place in the wall where I'd accidentally punched a hole through it. I was trying to show my dad some karate moves I'd learned. Well, self-taught from watching a movie, which would explain what happened next. My hand went right through the drywall.

"You'll need a license for those, little girl," he'd said as he excused himself to the garage, returning with supplies to repair it.

"Ready to go?" Audrey said, breaking me out of my memory.

"I guess." I felt my throat tighten. "I know I wanted this for them, and I still believe it's for the best, but wow, I'm going to miss this place."

"Me too." She hugged me.

We locked the house and then took one more look before driving away. On the way, we drove through Jumpin' Beans for coffee.

"What's the deal with you and Eddie?" she asked after we got our order.

"What do you mean?" I could feel my face was going to give me away.

"You two are into each other, aren't you?"

"No, no. We're just friends."

"That was almost believable. I mean, if I didn't know you so well, I might actually believe it."

"It's just a little crush. Nothing more."

"A little more believable, but really sell it this next time," she teased.

"Oh, hush. Seriously, it's nothing. We went to lunch the other day, as friends, and nothing more."

I stared out the window, hoping for the end of the conversation. I didn't want to think about Eddie, especially when I still wasn't sure what my relationship with Clint was going to look like. He'd proposed to me after all.

"Fine, fine. I can tell you don't want to talk about this." She switched lanes. "Anything fun going on in the medium world for you?"

"Nothing too exciting." I whipped around. "Though there is a murder case."

"Do tell!"

"Do you remember hearing about those two guys that passed recently at Birdsong?"

"Uh-oh, don't tell me that the place we've just sent our parents to live at has a murderer running around."

"Okay. I won't tell you. I'll just smirk from over here."

"Damn, Joanna! Do you think they're safe?"

"Yes, they should be fine." I was almost positive about that. "These guys were both loaded. Like tech money big. Almost Bill Gates level."

"Wow. You think that's why they were killed?"

"Maybe. I honestly don't know yet." I turned towards her. "The crazy part is, they both left their estates to Kelli."

"Wait? Kelli-Kelli? As in the event coordinator at the place we're moving our parents to?"

"Yes, but I don't believe it was her. Too obvious. Plus, she's so sweet to all the residents."

"Yeah, sweet people never just snap."

I rolled my eyes at her sarcastic tone. "I think it was one of the jealous women there, honestly. Not Kelli."

"There do seem to be a lot of hormones and rage going on around there. You would think women that age would be over it."

"So true."

We pulled up. Audrey punched in the gate code so we could drive right up to their apartment. A few residents who were out walking waved as we drove by.

Then as we rounded the corner to their building, we saw the moving trucks. Hank's crew had them about half unloaded.

"They're good," Audrey said. "I will never hire any other moving company."

"I didn't exactly hire this moving crew. They were nicely forced upon us."

"Yeah, but still." She nodded towards the nearly empty trucks and the many helping hands. She parked the car in a visitor spot and then we went to find Mom and Dad.

"They're inside," one of the ladies on Hank's team said. I'd missed her name. Something like Nikki or Nicole or maybe Natasha. Something with an N.

"Thanks," I said over my shoulder as we headed in.

Inside the apartment was a mess of people and boxes everywhere. I saw Hank directing his team from a chair set in the living room. I could hear Mom and Dad as well as another voice.

"Oh, hey, Jo, Audrey," my dad said, coming out of the bedroom. "Your mom and Phyllis are in there."

He kissed us both as he went to join Hank. I could hear the two men start talking about poker. The next sound I heard was my mom's laughter. It wasn't a sound we heard often, and my sister and I both looked at each other.

"Is she really laughing?" Audrey asked with a giggle.

"I think so."

I hadn't heard that sound in years. It was nice. I was feeling like I'd pushed them in the right direction despite the couple of murders here.

"Oh, hey, girls," Mom giggled when we walked in.

"Hi, ladies," Phyllis greeted us with a smile.

They were unpacking clothes.

"Wow, you already have some empty boxes in here." Audrey peeked into a few.

Being the overachiever, she grabbed a box cutter and started breaking them down.

"Yes, we've been making great progress, and thanks to Hank, we should be nearly settled in by tonight," Mom grinned.

Nikki or Nicole or whatever her name was came in with a small box. "It says bathroom?"

"Oh, thanks Naomi. That goes in this one." Mom pointed to the main bathroom in their room.

Naomi. That's her name, I thought.

They'd gotten a two-bedroom with one and a half bathrooms, which should be perfect for them. Mom could have her crafting room and Dad had the extra toilet. Win-win.

There was a knock on the door and then several female voices. We walked out to see Odette, Robin, Kelli, and another woman I hadn't met before.

"Hi, y'all," Odette gushed. "We're the welcoming committee!"

"We just want to welcome you both to the Birdsong family. We look forward to many years of friendship," Robin said.

"Well, thank you," Dad said. "I'm Charlie, and this is Babs, then our girls Audrey and Joanna. They're just helping us get moved in."

"Nice to meet you. I'm Odette." She smiled at me since we'd already met. "This is Robin and Heidi, and then you've met Kelli, right?"

"Yes, hi, nice to meet you all and see you again, Kelli," Mom said.

That's when Phyllis came out of the bedroom. She and Odette locked eyes. The tension in the air could be cut with a knife. Even some of Hank's crew backed out slowly.

"What are you doing here?" Odette snapped.

"Helping my new friends move in," Phyllis hurled back.

"Babs, Charlie, I will give you one piece of advice. Don't hitch your wagon to this, this hussy! She will steal your man," Odette wagged her finger at my dad, "and then throw him away and he dies with a broken heart."

There was a gasp from the room, except from Robin, who added, "She has no feelings and look at how she dresses. Just like a teenybopper. Act your age!"

"How dare you? Both of you!" Phyllis took a step forward. "I have no interest in your man, men, whatever. I am here to live out my years and enjoy it with friends." She looked over at Mom, then stepped forward. "Babs has been the best friend I've had in years, so don't come in here with your clique and try to steal another friend from me."

"We didn't steal Alma Jean. She came running!" Odette growled.

Ah, another piece of the puzzle.

"Yeah, she didn't want to be attached to you and your wily ways," Robin snipped.

"Wily ways? Y'all have no argument. You just hate me because you ain't me." She flipped her silvery hair.

Odette lunged forward, but Kelli stopped her. "Ladies, ladies.

That's enough. There's no reason for this behavior. You don't have to like each other or even be friends, but at least don't drag others into it. Babs and Charlie are new here and this is not the welcome that Birdsong wants to extend them."

"No, you're right." Odette grabbed the gift basket from Heidi and shoved it at my dad. "Welcome to Birdsong," she said through tight lips. "Come on, ladies."

The three older ladies turned on their heels with a huff and a humph over their shoulders as they stormed out. Kelli watched them go and then turned with a frown.

"I'm so very sorry about them. I have no idea what's gotten into them." She reached her hand out to Mom. "Please know that not everyone here is like them. They're just the loudest voices at the moment."

She smiled at Phyllis and then nodded a goodbye.

"See why they need such a good security company here," Hank said with a chuckle, and then he directed his team to get back to work.

"I'll be right back," I mumbled to Audrey, then I went to find Kelli.

I found her in one of the nearby gardens having a heated discussion with the other three ladies. I couldn't quite hear what they were saying, but I could tell it had everything to do with what had just happened.

They saw me and nudged each other to look my way.

"Sorry, I didn't mean to interrupt." I gave a weak smile to the group.

"What do you want?" Odette snapped.

I didn't know what I'd done to her, but okay.

"I was hoping to speak with Kelli for a moment."

"Of course." Kelli gestured for me to follow her.

We walked to her office and then she had me take a seat.

"Sorry about those ladies. There's just a lot of history between the two sides."

"What is it all about? And don't tell me guys because..." I stopped myself before I spilled the beans about talking to Jack and Ruben.

"You think they're too old to be acting like that, right? Me too."

"Yeah, is that normal?"

"They're really the only group that acts like this. Sure, there are a few others that have a little drama among them. Disputes over parking spots, gardens, and it all boils down to jealousy. But something about Phyllis makes the others act like middle school girls fighting to be the queen bee or something."

"I hate that my parents are getting caught up in it. I thought this move would be good for them."

"Oh, I'm sure they'll be fine here as long as..."

I stopped her before she could finish. "As long as they stop being friends with Phyllis."

She'd already told me this once, but it seemed just as queen bee-ish to me. Don't be friends with her or else.

"Sadly, yes."

"Definitely mean girl behavior."

"Yes, sad but true." She frowned but then smiled. "That isn't what you wanted to talk to me about, was it?"

"Oh, no, it wasn't. I wanted to ask you about Ruben and Jack a bit. How well did you know them?"

"Oh, I knew them really well. They were like father figures to me. I didn't really know my own and neither of them had children." She laughed. "I have a lot of 'adoptive' parents here, especially the lonely ones with little or no family."

"That's nice. I'm sure it makes you all happy to have each other."

"Yes, but it's hard." She sniffed and grabbed a tissue. "It's hard when they pass. We get so close and spend a lot of time together, then they're gone. It really leaves a gap."

"I can imagine."

"But I did know getting close to them meant a risk of getting hurt. I mean, life is short and none of us know how long we have." She smiled. "Is there anything else?"

I hesitated a moment. Should I ask her about enemies or someone who hated them? It might tip her off to the investigation, and even though I didn't suspect her, I didn't think I could trust her.

"Well, just one more. Were there other friends of theirs here? People they hung out with?"

"Why? Is there something going on? Have you talked to them?"

"No, not yet. Just curious in case they ever do come to me. I'd know where to find them." That was believable, right? I flashed a perfect stage smile.

She eyed me, then smiled. "They played poker most of the time with those guys. Damon, Henry, and Felix."

"Okay, well, that's helpful, you know, just in case." I tried to be casual and breezy about it.

"Well, great. I have to get over to the community room. We have to get set up for a party later today. We do a once-a-month birthday party for the residents with birthdays during that month."

"Oh, that sounds like a lot of fun."

"It is. They always enjoy it."

I stood, thanked her again, and then hurried back to my parents' new apartment.

Chapter Nineteen

Mom and Dad had been at Birdsong now for about a week, so today I was going to check in with them and see how they were settling in.

Thanks to Hank's team being so amazing, Mom and Dad had gotten unpacked in record time. Then the crew had cleared most of the empty boxes and various moving debris.

They'd been the best movers a person could have, but especially Naomi, who stayed behind and helped Mom and Phyllis unpack the kitchen, get it organized, and clean up. I was happy to have met her, and I would be sure to remember her name next time.

I got Oakley up, dressed, and fed. We took Chewy on a quick walk before heading over there. On our drive, I checked my rearview mirror more than was probably necessary. A habit I'd gotten into since I met Jeremy Landon more than a year ago. I'd been followed too many times to count. This was the point in my investigations when that would start.

No car caught my attention as suspicious. Good.

So far, nothing much had happened with this one, and that made me almost more nervous than when I was being actively stalked or having my house broken into. It gave a false sense of safety and comfort, which meant the hammer might fall at any moment.

I thought about our encounter with the so-called Welcoming Committee the other day. They'd been less than welcoming when they found out that Phyllis was there. It made me think we were on the right track with one of them being a suspect.

My limited knowledge of them, none of those ladies drove any longer, so less risk of one of them harassing me, at least.

Which reminded me, I didn't see Clint yesterday. I wondered what happened with their search warrants.

"I should call him, don't you think?" I said out loud.

"Da?" Oakley asked.

"Um." Should I allow her to keep saying that? She only knew to call him by that name, so fine for now. I didn't know how to explain things to her, so I'd let it go. "Yes, should we call him?"

"Da! Da!" She kicked her feet.

"I'll take that as a yes." I hit the button for Clint.

Oakley started singing in the backseat.

"Hello," came his deep voice over the car speakers.

"Da! Hi, Da!"

"Hi, Oakie-girl. How are you?" he cooed.

She giggled and then began babbling. He answered with the appropriate number of "oh, yeah?" and "really?" among other random comments.

She seemed happy with the conversation when she said bye and began singing again.

"I guess she's done with you," I laughed.

"It sounds like it. So, I'm assuming that's not why you called."

"No, I wanted to find out how the interviews went at Birdsong. I didn't see you, so I wasn't sure."

"Oh, yeah, that. We were denied the search warrants until we can provide a better case than a ghost told us." His tone was the equivalent of an eye roll.

I did roll my eyes at his attitude. "You do have an autopsy that shows murder. Is that enough?"

"Yeah, but without probable cause, meaning more of a suspect, we can't just go barging in without a few more facts." He sighed. "I'm still working on it. I haven't given up. It's clear he was murdered and I believe you."

"Oh my, did Detective Hartley just admit to believing in my psychic powers? I better watch out for flying pigs."

"Ha, ha. Yes, I've had a hard time believing this stuff, but it's difficult to argue with the results, even if sloppy at times."

"I'll take that as a compliment, so thank you."

"But the short answer to your original question is, I didn't get to interview any of the women yet, but I'm hoping to get this search warrant updated and then we can go do the search and interviews."

"Why can't you just go talk to them?"

"If one of them did kill both men, we don't want to tip them off before we can find evidence. They could easily hide nicotine and anything else we might need to find our suspect."

"Ah, yes, that makes sense. I won't tip anyone off for sure. We're actually heading over there now to see how my parents are getting settled in."

I thought back to my conversation with Kelli last week. I hoped I hadn't blown things by talking to her. I'd tried to be casual and calm while talking to her. I wasn't going to tell Clint, just in case though. He would be pissed.

"Okay, good." He paused. "Obviously, keep this between us."

"Of course."

"Well, let me know how things are over there and I'll call you soon so we can get coffee or something."

"Sounds good."

After we hung up, I thought about what he said. It did make sense to not tip off the murderer to our investigation, but there was no guarantee that they hadn't already thrown it all out, unless they had more plans.

Again, I hoped I hadn't messed things up. I'd tried to be careful with my words.

That thought sent a chill through my body. I couldn't even think about that now with my parents there. It was another reason I was going over today, just to ensure they were all good.

We pulled up, and I punched in the gate code.

"Are you ready to see Gramma and Grampa?" I asked.

"Gam. Papa." She cheered.

I was so thankful she loved them as much as they loved her. It had always been a slight worry when I'd started the adoption process and it happened so quickly that I didn't even get to talk to them about it. But they were open and welcoming in every way, and what's not to love when you welcome a new baby?

I parked in a spot near my parents' unit and then got the cheering baby out of her seat. My mother met us halfway.

"There's my little girl." She reached out for the lunging toddler.

"Mwah!" Oakley said, giving her grandmother a big, sloppy kiss.

"Ha, when did she start saying mwah as part of the kiss?"

"A few days ago."

Mom smiled. "Well, y'all, come on in."

Stepping in, it was like an almost different place.

"Wow, Mom, it looks like you've been living here for weeks. Looks great."

"Thanks." She looked around. Her late eighties decor somehow looked refreshed and less mauve in this space. "Phyllis gave me some design and decorating tips. It's a work in progress."

"It's great." I took a seat on the sofa. "Where's Dad?"

"At the putting greens with a few new friends."

"Oh, that's nice. I'm glad for him. Where's Phyllis today?"

"She's visiting her daughter. She'll likely be back late tonight or early in the morning. She wasn't sure."

"That's nice." Then I noticed my mom's shiny red nails. My mom was a barely there, nudes, pale pinks lady all my life, but here she was with fire engine red polish. "Mom, your nails."

"Oh, don't you just love them! Kelli has a salon team come in twice a month to give treatments. I got a pedicure and manicure."

She slipped her flats off and flashed me the same red polish on her toes.

"Love them! That color is fun."

"It is fun, isn't it? I'm so glad Phyllis encouraged me to try something new."

"Me too, and I'm happy to hear you're enjoying it here."

"It's wonderful! I'm thankful we found this place."

I bit my tongue, resisting the urge to tell her I found this for her. It had been enough of a challenge to get her to even consider it, let alone look, so that was not worth the battle.

Oakley toddled over to her grandmother and handed her a book. They began reading it together.

"So, when is Dad going to be back? Did you want to do lunch?"

"Yeah, I made chicken salad and picked up croissants to put it on."

"I love your chicken salad."

"I know you do." Mom smiled at me.

Who was this woman? I watched her play with her granddaughter. Then after Oakley got bored, Mom showed me around.

"It really does look great, Mom. This craft room is laid out almost better than in the house."

"Yeah, I think so. It feels more efficient."

Oakley started to get into things she shouldn't, so we decided to take her for a walk around the community. We were greeted by a number of other residents who gushed over the little visitor.

"Babs, she is just the cutest thing," one lady said. "Hi, Joanna, I never got to thank you for doing a reading for me that day. It was nice to hear from my sister."

"Oh, you're welcome."

"Hello, Babs!" Another lady came up to us. "Who is this little darlin'?"

"This is my granddaughter, Oakley." My mom beamed.

"Well, isn't she just the sweetest thing?"

Oakley would flash her sweet toothy grin at all the ladies. She would sometimes giggle and say hi. Then a man came by with a dog.

"Dawg!" Oakley yelled and took off running.

Thankfully she wasn't fast yet and still mostly toddled, so I could catch up to her quickly. I was able to grab her before she got too close.

The little dog jumped and barked, but its tail wagged wildly. It seemed friendly, though. Going forward, this was going to be a struggle until I could fully explain to her about dogs.

"Is your dog friendly?" I asked.

"He is, and he especially loves children."

I put Oakley down and she began patting the dog and babbling to him. He licked her and wagged his tail even faster if that was possible. By then Mom had caught up to us. She simply smiled at the gentleman.

"You're Joanna, the Medium, right?"

My mom rolled her eyes.

"Yes, that's me, and this is Oakley, my daughter, and my mother, Babs. She and my father, Charlie, just moved in."

"Oh, nice. Welcome to you. I think I met Charlie. He's over at the putting greens right now with Henry and Damon." He then turned to me. "You did a reading here a few weeks ago. I was so happy to hear from my son that day. It really gave my wife and me some peace."

"Oh, I'm so glad to hear. That's what I try to do." I smiled as I watched my daughter playing with the puppy. "What's your pup's name?"

"Barnaby. He's a dachshund. Actually, my wife's dog, but she's playing bingo right now, and he needed a walk."

Barnaby looked away and started barking excitedly. It looked like he was doing a dance in place and his tail was wagging so fast.

We followed his gaze. A group of women were walking towards us. I recognized a few of them.

"Hey, Barnaby baby. Mom's coming." It was Heidi from the Welcoming Committee who didn't speak that day. She was with Odette and Robin. "Oh, hi, Joanna."

"Hi, ladies." I smiled at the group but tried not to make eye contact with my mother.

I could feel her tension without looking. Odette gave a tight-lipped smile while Robin just mumbled something. Heidi looked at her companions with confusion.

"Heidi, right? Your dog is so adorable. My daughter just loves dogs."

"Aw, she's so precious." Heidi squatted down to address Oakley. "Do you like the doggy?"

"Yes. Dawg. Ball?"

The ladies chuckled. A slight icebreaker.

"Yes, he has a ball. Do you want me to go get it?"

"Ball! Yes. Ball." She pointed in a direction.

"Do you have time?" Heidi looked at me.

"Um, sure." I looked at my mother, who simply nodded.

"Great. We're just over this way." She gestured to a unit nearby.

We followed Heidi and Felix along with the unwelcoming committee and my now pouting mother. At least Oakley was happy. She toddled right along with Barnaby, babbling to him about the ball. When we got to their unit, Felix excused himself.

"I'm going to catch up to the guys on the putting green and maybe see if any of them want to play a few hands of poker." He winked at his bride as he left.

Heidi grabbed two small tennis balls and suggested we go to the open area outside. She then unhooked the dog's leash and handed a ball to Oakley.

"Go, dawg!" She said as she threw it, and then it was on. She and Barnaby chased around. Heidi occasionally grabbed one ball or another to keep it in play.

While we watched, the two stoic members of the welcoming committee fidgeted and gave us both side-eye.

"Umm, Babs, right?" Odette finally said.

"Yes, that's right." My mother's acidic tone wasn't a surprise after how these ladies acted towards her the other day.

"Sorry about the other day. I just didn't expect her to be there," Odette offered.

"Yes, well, thank you." Mom adjusted her posture. "She has been helpful and welcoming to me and my family."

Odette cleared her throat and looked at Robin before speaking again.

"We just haven't gotten off to the best start with her and, you know, I'm not going to beat a dead horse here. Just that we want to welcome you to the Birdsong community." She paused, clearing her throat again. "Would you both like to join us for lunch? We were going to eat in the cafeteria."

Odette half-smiled, then looked over at the other two ladies, who then looked at my mother and me.

"We actually have plans already, but perhaps another day."

"Oh, great," Robin said through a tight smile. "We look forward to it."

My mother gave her famously fake smile and a once-over look. You would have to know her to really catch the subtle move, but I did and had to look away before I blew her whole ruse by giggling.

We all watched Oakley and Barnaby play for another minute before both groups got back on track. We went back to my parents' apartment and the other ladies headed to arts and crafts with Kelli before their lunch.

"I do not like those ladies much," Mom said as we got out of earshot.

"But you're going to lunch with them one day?"

"Nope. It was just a polite thing to say, not what I really wanted to say to them."

"Which was?"

"They can stick their invite where the sun don't shine." She completed the sentence with a quick thrust upwards with her finger.

"Oh, Mom, you are amazing." I laughed.

She simply grinned as we stepped into her apartment. Once

again, I was seeing my mother in a new light, but this time, I really liked her and her red nails.

Chapter Twenty

~ Clint ~

We finally got the green light to interview the suspects at Birdsong. Monday morning, and we were putting our tactical teams together.

"Alright. Buckley and Wright, y'all will go to Odette's apartment. Hartley and I will take Robin's place, and Williams and Gomez, you have Phyllis." Terry read off our clipboard planning sheet.

"What about Dawn?" Wright asked.

"Ah, yes..." Terry ran his finger down the page. "Ugh, we didn't get a warrant for Dawn. Where is the warrant?"

I pulled out our stack of paperwork. Not there.

"Shit." I mumbled. This close. We needed to interview all of them at once.

Chief came barging into the room. "Trouble at Birdsong. Multiple victims, mostly just ill, but I've heard two deceased. Looks like our killer has poisoned a mass number of residents. This is an all-hands op." He started calling additional officers.

"Do you have any names?" My mind immediately went to Jo's parents. They'd only been moved in for about a week now.

"None yet. We need to get there and get more details, but the EMTs have already been transporting to the hospital. They're the ones that tipped us off when they realized the magnitude of what had happened."

Our meeting ended as everyone poured out of the conference room. We all grabbed gear from our respective desks and headed to the cars.

I stared mindlessly at my phone. "I don't know if I should call Jo or wait until I know more."

"Wait. I'm sure if something is going on with her parents, she already knows. If not, we can call her then."

"True."

I tried to be calm and not fidget too much as we drove. The usual fifteen-minute drive felt twenty times longer, but I'm sure it was just my nerves.

We arrived at the senior community to find controlled chaos. Ambulances lined the long driveway and into the right-side gate. Our team turned left into the visitor lot. As we got out of our cars, we had a team set a perimeter to keep the media at bay. We knew they'd be here any moment.

Next, we got with the lead EMT to find out what she knew.

"We have a few dozen sick residents and two deceased. The ME is on his way to assess them." She handed us a list. "I got this from the main office. Highlighted in yellow are those already transported to the hospital, in green are those we're loading now, and no highlight means not impacted."

I tried scanning the list for the Webbers, but it was long.

"Do you have names of the deceased?" I knew I shouldn't ask yet, but I had to know.

"Hartley, you know until Doc gets here, I can't give you that." She winked at me.

I wasn't in the mood to flirt. I needed to know if Charlie and Babs were involved.

"Yeah, I just know two of the residents really well, and I want to confirm they're still safe."

She sighed. "Names?"

"Charles and Barbara Webber."

"Oh, Joanna's folks!" Of course she knew Joanna. She was a semi-celebrity in town. "No, they're fine. Shook up like many, but they're safe in their apartment. We asked all the residents not ill to stay in their homes until we got all the sick out."

"Great. Thank you so much."

Terry left to greet the media who'd just arrived. He'd lay the ground rules and let them know he'd give an interview once we had more information. That was his job.

I gathered our team from the meeting earlier.

"Alright, we have Odette and Robin at the hospital, so we can probably remove them from our suspect list, at least for now. Phyllis is unaffected, so we need to interview her. Dawn is also okay, so let's talk to her as well. And then we can divide up some of these others."

Terry joined me again, and together we went to talk to Phyllis first while Buckley and Gomez went to speak with Dawn.

Phyllis was our top suspect at this point. We'd likely take her to the station and have a team comb through her apartment for evidence.

I knocked on her door. I don't know who I expected to answer, but the woman in front of me was stunning and interesting in a way I hadn't anticipated for a seventy-year-old woman. More like a thirty-something.

She wore ripped jeans and a faded KISS concert t-shirt. Her hair was cut all the same length, hanging just to her shoulder. Simple, and that made her look stunning.

"Phyllis King?" Terry said.

"Yes, that's me." She frowned. "You're probably here thinking I did all this, right? Rumors are a bitch, aren't they." She looked over her shoulder, then opened the door wide. "Come on in while I get my shoes and purse."

My mouth fell open. Again, I hadn't expected the woman to be so cooperative.

We stepped inside. This was nothing like my grandparents' or older family members' homes. It was hip and modern. Bright, abstract artwork hung on the walls, and the furniture was soft and funky, both in color and shape. Most people I knew in their seventies had furniture left over from the late eighties that was more about form and function, not fun and funky.

"Make yourselves at home." She sat down in a bright red wooden chair and slipped on her combat boots.

Terry cleared his throat. "We can ask you a few questions here, but as you've already guessed, we'll be taking you to the station and we'll have a team come in to search for evidence." He handed her the search warrant.

"So this was already in motion before all of this mess?"

"Yes."

"Those ladies sure do have it out for me. Once all this is cleared up, I'll probably move somewhere else. It's a shame, though, because I really liked it here, at least for the most part." She sat back. "What's the first question?"

"Where were you yesterday?"

"With my daughter. I was there most of the weekend. She brought me home early this morning. In fact, I arrived just minutes before the first ambulances arrived."

"Alright." Terry made a note.

I shifted from one foot to the other as I fidgeted internally, and a bit externally. I really just wanted to go see Charlie and Babs, to ensure they were fine, and then to connect with Joanna. She had to have heard by now, and I wanted her to know we were on it.

Terry gave me a pointed look.

"Okay, we'll just need to verify that with your daughter and any others that can back up your alibi."

"Not a problem. I know where I've been and what I have and haven't done." She grabbed her purse and handed me the keys. "Make sure your folks lock up. As you can see, there are people out to get me."

She stepped out into the walkway but stayed in plain sight.

Terry looked around briefly, then turned to me. "Are you okay?"

I peeked towards the open door where Phyllis stood waiting. "I'm just worried about the Webbers, and of course Jo is going to be beating herself up for this. Well, not this exactly, but having her parents move here with this going on."

"As soon as we get all the suspects or potential suspects accounted for, we'll check on them."

I nodded, and together we walked out. Phyllis went with Officer Williams, who would escort her to the station for us. We headed to Dawn Holmes' apartment to catch up with the other officers.

Nobody was there. The officers were standing outside waiting.

"Not here, Detectives." The officer said when we arrived.

"Is she on the list?" Terry asked.

I ran through the list. "Yes, but not highlighted. Beth Ann said those not highlighted would be in their apartments." I made a note.

"Guilty, or maybe overlooked as being one of the sick?"

"Obviously no idea, but we can find out."

I looked around as I tried to think of what we should do next. We needed to go back to the front and touch base with the EMTs. We also needed to find Dr. Starke, and we still needed to interview as many residents as possible.

"Should we just go to as many residents as we can then? Not trying to find these suspects since the rest are at the hospital?"

"I feel like we're just grasping at straws with that method, but

I don't have a better solution, so let's do it."

We had the other two officers go back to the main command center to find out where Dawn was.

Then we did the divide and conquer thing to cover more ground. I handed Terry half of the list, and we headed off in two different directions.

An hour later, I'd talked to a dozen or so people. Everyone pointed to a different person, but most said Phyllis. Emotionally, I was drained, but I had to finish.

"She's a troublemaker and always in the middle of everything." One lady said.

"She isn't any worse than that Odette and her sidekicks. Always sticking their nose in everyone's business." Her neighbor added.

"Yeah, but Odette and Robin are both in the hospital. Phyllis isn't."

"That's true. I guess I change my answer to Phyllis as well."

"There aren't any others that had a problem with Jack Reynolds or Ruben Harper? Anyone who seems to not like this many people?" I was at a loss for words at this point. My body felt heavy as the emotional fatigue set in.

"Oh, no, they were both so well liked. Poor Kelli was devastated when they passed. They were father figures to her."

"Kelli? The Event Coordinator."

"Yes, she was always spending time with them, helping them with groceries or playing cards. They'd really taken to her, called her their daughter. Well, not theirs together, but ya know, just the daughter neither of them had." The first lady said.

"Yeah, she's a daughter to many of us, but some more than others."

That gave me a thought. "Thank you both. This has been helpful."

"I hope you catch this person. I love our cafeterias, and if it isn't safe, what will I eat? I don't cook any longer."

I simply nodded and smiled as I walked away. Terry was just finishing up, so I waited a few yards away.

"Well, thank you, Mr. and Mrs. Carter. This has been helpful." He turned and saw me, but waited until he was away from the resident's door before asking, "Did you find something?"

"Maybe. That Kelli has a strong relationship with the deceased. Perhaps we should look closer at her?"

"She's in the hospital at the moment too. ICU." He frowned.

"Well, damn." My shoulders dropped. "I'm out of ideas."

"We should regroup with the team that's looking through Phyllis' apartment."

"And I probably need to check in with Joanna and her parents."

We agreed to meet back up outside of the main office in about thirty minutes or so. I pulled out my phone and saw I had a missed call and voicemail from Joanna. After listening to it, I headed towards her parents' unit.

Dread set in with each step. I didn't have any answers, and I knew they'd want them.

Chapter Twenty-One

I was working in my office between appointments, doing one of my favorite parts of this job, which was answering client emails. These messages of appreciation, hearing the hope and love from clients, always put a smile on my face. It was the reason I loved doing this, especially now that it was real again.

I hit send on the email I'd just typed, then reached for my coffee mug.

Empty.

My face fell a bit. It's always disappointing and annoying, thinking there's one more sip only to find nothing but emptiness.

I sighed and pushed up from my desk so I could get a refill. When I walked in, four heads turned to stare at me. The faces belonged to Percy, Micah, Tessa, and Josh. I didn't even know when Josh had arrived or that he was coming today.

"What're y'all doing in here?" I laughed, thinking they were goofing off. "Don't we have work to do?"

Nobody laughed as they turned back to the television.

"There's something happening at Birdsong, but we don't know much yet." Tessa mumbled.

Gasping, I turned my focus to the news report.

"Roughly a dozen residents have been taken to the hospital for intense stomach pain and vomiting. We have heard two residents have passed away," the reporter was saying.

I ran out of the room, back to my office. My parents had only been there a week. I was there just yesterday. Guilt hit me like a ton of bricks while I looked around for my phone.

"Where is it?" Frantically searching around my desk, slamming and throwing things, before finally remembering it was in my purse.

On my knees, I threw the drawer open, then rummaged through my purse in search of the phone. Finding it, I saw I had missed six calls and roughly fifteen text messages between my parents and my sister. Why hadn't they tried our office number?

With shaking hands, I pushed the button for my mom.

"Joanna! Where have you been?" She blurted without even a hello.

"What's happening over there? Are you and Dad okay?"

"We're okay, but so many people are sick. Some didn't need to go to the hospital, but so many others did." She sniffed. "They're still here assessing people to determine if they need to go to the hospital. We have to stay in our apartments for now."

"Do they know what happened?"

"Something about poison in the food. I don't know all the details yet."

I could hear her voice cracking, clearly flustered and distraught. It broke my heart and made me feel guilty. Had I put my parents in even more danger than a fall from a ladder?

"Do they have any idea what or how?"

"No, but I've heard they arrested several people, including Phyllis."

"Arrested? Mom, are you sure?"

I didn't think they could actually arrest anyone unless there was probable cause. Isn't that why the search warrants had been denied? Clint had said they could interview but hadn't wanted to spook the culprit, so that's why they'd hesitated.

But maybe that meant they'd found something. Enough to make arrests.

"I don't know. They took them to the station for interviews and said something about search warrants." She sighed. "You know I don't know all that police jargon."

"Okay, okay. I'm on my way. Call me if anything changes." I grabbed my purse as we ended the call.

I ran back to the break room. They were all still in there, glued to the news.

"I need to go check on my parents. They either arrested Phyllis or are interviewing her, but you know Mom. She doesn't always get the facts just right." I blurted.

Tessa followed me as I made my way out the front door.

"Of course. I'll cancel the rest of your clients and get them scheduled for a free session." Tessa said, hugging me quickly. "Let me know if you need anything, and I mean anything."

"Thank you. I will."

I tried to stay calm and drive the speed limit, but my brain was distracted by the potential danger my parents were in. I hit the button for Audrey.

"Jo, what's going on at Birdsong?"

"I don't know, but I'm heading there now to find out."

"I wish I could come with you, but I don't want to take the boys, and Stan is in a meeting at the moment, so he can't come home yet. Call me when you know something, and I'll head over as soon as Stan can get here to be with the boys."

"Of course."

Next, I dialed Clint's number. It rang, then went to voicemail. Perhaps he was busy. I hoped he and Terry were on the case. I left a quick message to let him know I was on my way to check on my folks.

As I pulled up at Birdsong, I saw a number of police cars and ambulances. Of course, I was stopped at the gate.

"My parents live here. Charles and Barbara Webber." I told the officer.

She ran her finger down the list, then looked up. "Wait, you're Joanna, right?"

"That's right."

"Go ahead." She gestured to another officer, who opened the gate for me to go through. I drove around and parked as close as I could get to their apartment. Once parked, I practically sprinted to their unit.

"Mom? Dad?" Then I saw them sitting together at the kitchen table. Mom had a pile of tissues in front of her. I joined them, putting my arm around my mom. "You okay?"

"They have Phyllis down at the station right now interviewing her, and I don't know what's happening." She grabbed up a couple more tissues. "People are saying she added the poison to the food, but that's ridiculous. She wasn't even here yesterday."

"So they think it happened yesterday?" I sat back in the chair.

"Yes, and we ate all of our meals in our apartment, thank goodness." Dad said.

I'd had lunch with them, but if we hadn't, this could have easily been all of us, including Oakley.

"Well, that's definitely good. Remind me where Phyllis was?" I know Mom had told me yesterday.

"With her daughter all day. She came back early this morning." She sniffed.

I squeezed her hand. "When did people start getting sick?"

"Overnight and early this morning." She dabbed a tissue to her eyes. "I thought this was a safe place, and now we can't go home because a new family lives there, but this isn't safe either."

"We're safe here, Babs. I promise." My dad put his arms around her, but I could tell by his expression he wasn't sure if they were.

"Yes, of course you're safe."

There was a knock on the door. I stood to open it.

"Oh, Clint, hi."

"I got your message, then saw your car." He hooked his thumb over his shoulder.

"Ah. Well, come in."

"How're you doing?" He looked over at my parents.

"We're okay." My dad said, standing to greet Clint with a handshake. "Do you know anything about who did this?"

"Um, not yet. We have a few people we're talking to, but nothing concrete yet."

"Phyllis didn't do it." Mom blurted over Dad's shoulder.

Clint looked at her but didn't say anything for a moment. "We're listening to all the facts, and I'm sure we'll find the right person."

"I'll believe it when I see it." She retorted, then grabbed a couple of tissues as she started crying again.

"Well, I just wanted to check in on y'all." He said, then looked at me. "Can I speak to you outside?"

"Sure." I looked at my parents before stepping outside with Clint.

We walked away from their door. He leaned on the back of his truck that I hadn't seen here when I'd parked.

"Where's Terry?"

"He's checking with the officers in Phyllis' apartment, and then we'll be meeting up shortly. I excused myself to check on you." He looked at me. "You're good, though?"

"I think so. I just don't know what to think of all this. I feel so much guilt." I felt tears forming.

He pulled me into his chest, wrapping his arms around me. The warmth and comfort broke my resolve as the tears fell. He whispered to me, trying to comfort me, but I was a mess. The regret was too much.

"I just wanted them to be safe." I sobbed, clinging to him.

"I know, and they are. This is just a weird thing." He stroked my back as he spoke. "We'll figure out who's doing this, I promise."

"Thanks." I hiccuped a little. "Have you heard anything about Ruben Harper's autopsy yet?"

"Not yet, but should be soon. I did talk to Dr. Starke earlier to see if we could rush the results, especially given this incident."

I pulled back so I could talk more easily.

"Well, let me know, and if there's anything I can help with, let me know."

"You're good at getting people to talk, so maybe you can ask around without asking around, if you know what I mean."

"I can do that."

"Just please try to stay out of trouble." He said, wiping a tear from my face.

"I'll try my darnedest, but you know how it goes." I flashed a weak smile.

"I do." He looked at me. "I know I keep asking, but can we get together soon to talk?"

"I'd like that."

"I'll call you soon then, I promise."

I nodded and watched him walk away. He gave me a two-finger salute of goodbye as he turned the corner heading to meet Terry. I waved, then turned back to join my parents.

We kept saying we'd get together to talk soon, but it had yet to happen, and I was starting to think it was just a polite thing he was saying. I sighed, then opened the door to my folks' apartment.

"Did he say anything?" My mom asked the second I stepped in the door.

"Not really."

"Well, what good was his visit then?" She snapped and stomped off.

"She's just worried about all the sick folks and, of course, Phyllis." Dad apologized for her, like he'd done my whole life.

"I know."

I didn't take her snapping personally. She was clearly upset. So was I, but for somewhat different reasons. Though I was also worried about Phyllis. There wasn't much I could do today but try to figure out what was going on.

The restaurants and bistro on-site were closed until they could figure out who was able to access the food, what poison had been used, and, of course, how they'd been able to add it. My parents had a fully stocked kitchen and Mom loves to cook, so they were set. I thought of all the others who might not be.

I stayed with my parents for a few hours, but I had to get home for Oakley. I called Audrey on my way home to give her a quick update on both the folks and on Clint. Stan still hadn't been able to get out of work yet.

"So what are you going to do?" She asked when I was done with the debrief.

"I don't know yet. I know I'll need to talk to many of the residents, especially the sick ones."

"You'll have to wait until they get released from the hospital."

"Yeah, of course." I signaled to change lanes. "I have so much guilt over all of this."

"Why should you have guilt? Did you poison these people?

No. Someone else did that."

"You're right, but just Mom and Dad..."

"They're fine. Don't worry."

"You're right." I sighed. "If I hear anything new, I'll call you."

"Love you, sis."

"Love you, too."

I drove the rest of the way home, trying desperately not to beat myself up for pushing my parents and putting them in potential danger.

When I pulled in my driveway, I saw the dark SUV and knew that Hank was here. I parked next to it but didn't see anyone in the vehicle. Had Janie let him inside?

I headed in and was greeted by my favorite mutt.

"Hey, boy. Who's here?" I said, scratching his head, then stepping from the foyer around the wall into the living room. "Hello."

"Ma!" Oakley came running. "Look!"

She pointed to Hank and Al.

"I see them. Hello, Hank. Al." I nodded. "Where's my nanny?"

"We sent her home." Hank said. "I can watch this precious thing anytime."

I needed to talk to Janie about that, though I wasn't upset. She at least left them with people I trusted, especially Al. She knew that too.

I'd witnessed how he was with his sisters. Even though they were adults, he was so patient and gentle. Their special needs made them forever five years old in fifty-something-year-old bodies.

Still, she should have sent me a text to let me know. I looked down at my phone.

Oh, she did.

How had I missed it? Okay, angry moment over.

"Well, she seems to be having fun." I mumbled.

I watched as Oakley grabbed the ball and handed it to Al. He took it and threw it down the hall for Chewy, who took off after it, looking back to make sure the baby was chasing him. She was, giggling all the way.

"They've been doing this for the past ten minutes." Hank chuckled.

"They can do this for an hour or more." I said.

"I believe it."

Oakley got the ball back from Chewy and took it to Al to reset the game.

"So I know you didn't come all this way to watch my daughter play. What's going on?"

"Of course, though she is precious." He said, adjusting in his seat. "I'm sure you heard about the incident at Birdsong. Janie said you were there with your parents."

"I was. My mother is especially upset."

"I'm sure. Have you talked to the detectives yet?"

"I saw Clint for a moment, but he didn't know much. He said they'd been conducting interviews and combing through apartments."

"I'll speak with him. We can't have our citizens, especially our beautiful seniors, in danger like that. We have to protect them." He slammed his hands down on his thighs.

"I agree. I'm going to start talking to people to see what I can find out as well."

"Good, good. People like you, so they open up to you."

I'd been told this before, but it always surprised me when people said it. Even today when Clint mentioned it.

"Clint also said they should be getting Ruben Harper's autopsy back soon. They're asking the lab to try to prioritize it so they can compare the results from Jack Reynolds to his, and then to the poison in this case."

"Well, that's good. Very good." Hank sat back. "That's all I wanted to check on. We'll get out of your hair, but if you hear anything new, please be in touch."

Al said goodbye to Oakley.

"Bye-bye." She waved, then went right back to playing with just Chewy.

I plopped down on my couch with a heavy sigh, then cocked my head towards where the baby and dog were still playing.

This had been a crazy day, and I was just so grateful to be here with my little family. We were alive, healthy, and together. I couldn't ask for more at this moment.

Chapter Twenty-Two

A few days later, I took the afternoon off to visit some of the residents at Birdsong, including my parents. Most of the sick had been released, with only a couple of the critically ill still hospitalized, including Kelli. The residents were all, understandably, upset about their favorite staff member being nearly killed.

My plan for today was to talk to some of the victims, including Odette and Robin, who were initially suspects. I had a hard time thinking a person would poison themselves just to frame someone else, so I'd taken them off my suspect list.

Stranger things have happened, but these were little old ladies. They played dominoes and did crafts, had lunch together and gossiped about each other, but did that mean one of them was a killer?

Then there was poor Phyllis, who was staying with her daughter until this was solved. I couldn't explain why, but my gut feeling was she wasn't the killer. Not just because she'd welcomed my parents with open arms. It was simply intuition.

She hadn't been ruled out as a suspect, but as they couldn't find anything solid to hold her, they let her go with a warning to stay close.

Of course, my mother was distraught over losing her new best friend. I'd seen a shift in her since meeting Phyllis. She wasn't uptight or having her "headaches" any longer. She was laughing, joking, and wearing red nail polish.

But the last few days, she'd started to shift back to the old Babs. I wasn't a fan, not because of how she treated me, but for her overall happiness. I loved my mother, and I wanted her to have a good life.

I pulled up to the gate, punched in the code, and drove through. Even from inside my car, I could tell that the vibe here was different. The few people walking around didn't look up as I drove by. They didn't smile or wave like they had before. It was almost like zombies walking around.

A shiver ran up my spine. "What have I gotten into here?" I mumbled, pulling into the visitor spot closest to my parents' apartment.

Logically, I knew it wasn't my fault, but I still felt guilt at having pushed my parents to move here. I'd put them right in the middle of it.

"But how was I supposed to know this would happen?"

I sighed, grabbed my purse, and headed to their unit.

"Knock, knock," I said as I opened the door.

"Hey, Jo." Dad said.

He was kicked back in his recliner with the remote in one hand and a beer in the other. He started to get up. Even though he was mostly healed from the fall, he still wore a walking boot and had bad days with it.

"Hi, Dad. No, no, don't get up." I looked around. "Where's Mom?"

"She ran to the store."

"The car is here."

"Oh, yeah, she took the shuttle over with a few of the ladies."

"Which ladies?"

"I don't know. A few she just met."

"Not Odette or Robin, right?"

"No, she hates them." He chuckled.

I simply nodded and took a seat. My dad was watching a fishing show. I watched him instead of the television. He was really into this. I tried not to laugh.

"Do you know when she'll be back?"

"Not sure. Probably not too much longer."

"Alright. I'm going to go for a walk."

He smiled at me but didn't say anything, so I headed out the door that led to the courtyard and common areas.

I didn't see anyone as I stepped out. Odette lived in the same section as my folks and was the closest to where I was. Best to start with her.

I turned right at the end of the concrete hallway to the stairways, walked up to the second floor, then headed right again. Even though the hallways were not much to look at, each resident took the time to decorate the space around their doors. Currently, the doors were all decorated for either spring or St. Patrick's Day.

Some were as simple as a wreath on the door, while others

went all out with signs and plants that included woodland creatures dressed in holiday-appropriate gear. A small smile formed as I looked at each display.

As I neared Odette's unit, my smile faded. I didn't know what to expect out of this visit or if she'd even see me. I stopped to gather myself and take in her door decorations.

She'd decked it out for St. Patrick's Day with a small ceramic goose wearing a glittery green hat, green sparkly ribbons and bows in all her potted plants, and a bright green wreath on her door.

I took a deep breath and steadied my nerves before knocking. I heard her yell out from inside that she'd be right there, then the door opened.

"Oh. Hello, I wasn't expecting you." Her eyes looked hollow, and she had a paleness that told me she still wasn't feeling well.

"I'm sorry. I just wanted to see how you were feeling." I flashed my best stage smile. Though it was sincere, I simply needed her to believe I was, despite how we both felt about each other.

"I feel like someone tried to kill me." She snapped.

"Yeah, I'm sorry." I looked up and down the hallway. "Are you up for company?"

She studied me for a moment, then exhaled heavily. "Sure. Come in."

She stepped back so I could enter. Her home was nice and comfy. She had simple furnishings that looked as though she'd had them for many years. I bet there was a lot of history and memories in each item.

I smiled and turned towards her. "Your home is lovely."

She looked around. "Yeah? It looks like all the others around here. We downsize from our family homes, the ones we raised our children in and, in some cases, grandchildren too." She looked over at a framed picture. A deep frown crossed her face. "But then they all stop coming around, and we don't need a big house anymore, so we pick our favorite things and move into these retirement communities."

I forced a smile at her heartbreaking comment. She gestured for me to sit.

"Would you like a drink? I don't know what I have right now, but maybe water?"

"No, thank you."

She nodded and took a seat across from me.

"So how are you feeling, really?"

"I feel okay. Still worn out, but I hear I'm one of the lucky ones. Our poor Kelli nearly died." She reached for a tissue and dabbed her eyes.

"I heard a little bit. Do you know how she is now?"

"They say she'll make it and should be released soon, though I haven't heard if or when she'll be back to work."

"Do you remember that morning much? Like when did you know there was a problem, and any ideas on who could have done this?"

"What, are you a detective? I already answered their questions at the hospital."

"Oh, I'm sorry. Just curious because my parents live here now, and I want to keep them safe. And all of you safe." That was the truth, but only part of it.

"Well, if you can actually talk to ghosts, why don't you ask them about who did it?"

I'd tried, but the dead seemed to only see some things and not the important things. Perhaps what they saw was only important to them, like what their family was doing, but not what others did. It was strange, and I still didn't understand how this all worked.

Now, how was I going to explain this to her?

"I've tried before, but they don't always have answers."

"That doesn't make sense." She huffed. "You told me my husband knew that I was sleeping with other men."

"Well, I didn't say those words, exactly." She rolled her eyes as I spoke. "But yes, that's what he said, though I didn't want to completely embarrass you. It seems that the spirits only see some of what's happening. Whether they aren't around or they can't, I don't know."

"I guess that makes sense." She looked down. "Do you want to go with me to check on Robin? She isn't doing as well as me. They released her, but she's still really weak. I've been checking on her a few times a day."

"Yes, I'd love to see her." I smiled. "And I'm glad you're doing better too."

"Thanks." She mumbled.

As we walked, we made small talk about the different decorations and then about the gardens as we walked through one of the many flowered paths. We never got back to my questions about the how or who. That was okay. Maybe when we talked to Robin, they'd be more open together.

"With such a mild winter, it's amazing to see everything flowering like it has been." She said.

"Yes, I was surprised to see everything blooming too. My daughter loves to visit and smell all the flowers."

"She's adorable. Where is she now?"

"Thanks. She's with her nanny. I had to work today, then came straight here after."

"Well, word to the wise, always bring a little one. People here love to see children running around. It reminds us of our own."

"I saw the pictures in your apartment. How many children do you have?"

Her eyes clouded. "I had four. My oldest passed away, and I raised his children. They're grown now too."

"Oh, I'm sorry you lost your son, but what a blessing to be able to help with his children."

"I had to. His wife killed him."

My head whipped around at her apathetic tone. How could she say something like that with no emotion?

"Oh, um, I'm really sorry."

"It was a long time ago, and she was sentenced appropriately."

We reached Robin's door, so we didn't get a chance to finish discussing it more. Would I ever get to hear the full story? I doubted it, but if given a chance, I was going to find out.

She knocked softly, then opened the door. "Robin, are you awake?"

"I'm here." A weak voice came from the darkness.

"I have Joanna Webber here. Are you up for a short visit?"

"I guess." Her tone was snarky, or maybe she was just suspicious. I couldn't blame her for that.

"Hi, Robin. I just wanted to see how you're doing. I'm so sorry to hear what happened."

"Yes, well, we nearly died." She snarled, though it came out barely a whisper.

"I know. I'm hoping you can provide some information about the incident."

"Incident? The one where I almost died."

"She fancies herself a kind of detective, Robin." Odette snickered as she brought Robin a glass of water and a couple of pills. "These are just some pain relievers." She flashed them to me. "I'm no murderer."

"Of course. I mean, why would you be? Either of you. I just want to try to figure out who did so that we can keep y'all safe."

"And your parents." Odette added.

She hadn't exactly been polite to me at her apartment, but her tone had grown even cattier here with her friend. It was like they fed off each other with their attitudes. Not that I could blame them for being angry about the poisoning, but I didn't do it either.

"Yes, and any information you can give me could help."

"You aren't the police, so why should we help you?" Odette asked.

"I've worked with them on several cases, and I'm working with them on this one as well. I'm a consultant."

They both started laughing.

"My son told me all about what it means to be a consultant." Robin laughed. "He is one and says it just means he can charge whatever he wants to tell people they're wrong and why they should let him fix it for them."

I didn't know how to reply to that. These women were above anything and anyone I'd ever talked to, even Irene Crawford, the widow of the late Senator Crawford.

I cleared my throat. "Well, I guess if you aren't able to provide information, I'll excuse myself and go speak to other residents."

"No, no, sorry, Jo. May I call you Jo?" Odette asked. I simply nodded. "The only person all of this points to is that hussy Phyllis. The police have already interviewed her, and she isn't here anymore, which tells me she's guilty. She can't face us at all because of what she's done."

Robin nodded.

I just stared at them both. How could they believe that? But honestly, Phyllis was the only one in the middle of all the drama that hadn't gotten sick. I hated to say it, but it didn't look good.

"Well, maybe so." I smiled. "Thank you both for your time, and I hope you start to feel better soon, Robin."

I stood and left. I walked aimlessly for a moment, then found a group playing cards. I asked to join them and see what they knew about the incident.

An hour later, I realized two things. I was really bad at poker, and everyone just assumed it was Phyllis. They were no longer in danger.

"Ms. Joanna, anytime you want to join our game again, please stop by." One of the gentlemen said. I think his name was Henry.

"Thank you. If I ever need my ego taken down a peg, I'll be sure to join." The group chuckled.

"Yes, you are not good at poker." One of the other men said. Damon, I think.

I thanked them and went back to my parents' apartment to finish my visit and see if my mother had returned. Overall, I didn't think I'd learned a heck of a lot more than the police probably had.

"Where have you been?" My mom blurted when I walked in the door.

"I was playing cards with a few of the guys."

My dad laughed from the other room. "Did Damon and Henry get you roped into one of their games?"

I needed to get better at names.

"Yes, they're good."

"Who else was playing?"

"You know I'm bad at names sometimes. Frank, maybe? Jerry?"

"Probably Fred and Larry."

"Oh, yes, that's it."

"How can you not remember those names?" My mother snapped. "They're easy names."

I ignored her and changed the subject. "How was your shopping trip?"

"Not the same without Phyllis. I'll be glad when this is all cleared up. Though I doubt she'll stay here after all of this."

"That would be incredibly sad."

I wrapped up our visit shortly after that as I had to get home to Oakley, but I was glad to see my parents were doing okay. I'd gotten to talk to a few people, but I was still no closer to finding a murderer.

Chapter Twenty-Three

~ Joanna ~

We'd been taking a lot of Fridays off, so I decided we should just start working Monday through Thursday. Today was the first official Friday since making that change.

I was sipping coffee on the back patio, watching Chewy patrol the yard and Oakley play with the grass. My phone chimed.

It was Eddie. Weird.

Got time to chat?

Yes

My phone rang.

"Good morning."

"Good morning."

"Sorry to text so early, but I hoped you were awake."

"You got lucky. Just sitting here drinking coffee and watching the baby play outside."

"Do you mind if I stop by? I can bring donuts."

I laughed. "Tempting, but Eddie, I think we should just stay friends."

"That's what I want too."

"Are you sure?"

"Okay, the truth?"

"Please."

"Friends with the hope of being more."

"I'm sorry. I can't."

"Still in love with Hartley, huh?"

I knew it was true, but I wasn't about to admit it out loud.

"Yeah, I am."

"Well, lucky guy." He exhaled. "I can still bring you donuts if you'd like. Friends. Only friends."

"Donuts and a friend sound tempting, but I can't. I have some plans soon."

"I understand. We'll chat later then."

I sat there after we'd hung up, thinking about the conversation. It felt good to admit I still loved Clint, but it did little good if I didn't get a chance to tell him.

Today I had plans to visit Kelli. She'd just gotten out of the hospital, and I'd reached out to see if she'd be up for a visitor.

Micah and Josh were going to come stay with Oakley. She'd be so happy to see them later.

I finished my coffee, then got Oakley and Chewy back in the house. I dressed her for the day, then got myself ready.

There was a knock at the door.

"That must be Uncle Micah and Uncle Josh."

"Unc! Unc!"

Chewy went spinning and barking to the door.

"Hey, guys. Come on into party central." I said as I opened the door.

"Where's my favorite girl?" Josh said.

Oakley giggled and reached up to him.

"Hey, boss." Micah leaned over and kissed my cheek.

"Hey, thank you both for doing this for me today."

"Of course. Always happy to spend time with our favorite toddler." Josh said as he took her into the living room.

"And Chewy, of course," Micah added.

"Okay, so she's clean and fed. I should be home by lunchtime."

"Easy." Micah said, plopping down on my couch and tossing a ball to Chewy.

He caught it and dropped it in Micah's lap.

Oakley giggled. "Dawg ball!"

"Alright, well you know how to reach me if you need anything. Back soon."

I stopped at the store on my way over. I picked up a small plant for Kelli. Not knowing her likes or dislikes, I went with a beautiful succulent. It had purple, wide, waxy leaves and seemed happy to me. I hoped it would put a smile on Kelli's face too.

She lived close to Birdsong in a townhouse community near the new upscale mall and not far from downtown.

When I arrived, I buzzed her apartment at the gate.

"Hello?" came her voice over the intercom.

"Hey, Kelli. It's Joanna."

"Okay, opening the gate."

The gate in front of me jumped to life as it slowly slid open. I pulled forward and made my way down the row of homes.

They were a mix of stucco and stone in various colors. There was minimal landscaping in front of each home with just small stripes of grass.

I found Kelli's unit and parked behind her sedan. The door opened, and she stepped out. She looked pale, and her eyes looked sunken, hollow.

I waved from my car as I gathered my purse and plant.

"Good morning," I called as I stepped out.

"Good morning." Her voice was a bit hoarse. "Come on in. I just started a fresh pot of coffee."

"Sounds good."

I followed her inside. The house was dark with the blinds and curtains drawn. It was sparsely decorated with only a few pieces of furniture in each room.

Her office was so cheery with so many personal touches that I'd thought her home would reflect that. I was mildly shocked that it wasn't true, but I guess everyone had a different work versus home personality.

"I brought you a small get-well gift." I handed her the plant.

"Oh, thank you. It's so cute."

She gestured for me to sit as she stepped behind the kitchen counter. She selected two mugs, filling them both with coffee.

"Do you like cream and sugar?"

"Yes, please, just a touch of each."

She added them to my cup, then passed me the mug. She took a seat.

"How are you feeling?"

"Oh, I'm okay. That was scary, though."

"I can imagine." I didn't say that I'd had my own brushes with death. It was not fun in the least. But being on the other side was a blessing.

"I'm just glad that Phyllis is no longer at Birdsong."

"Is that official?"

"Well, I don't know, but for now at least, she isn't staying there."

"You think it was her?"

"It had to be, right? I mean, that's what the cops think."

"Yeah, but I think they may have other suspects."

"They do?" Her eyebrows raised.

Had I said too much?

"They didn't arrest her, so I just assumed. Honestly, I don't know."

"You used to date that detective, though, right? Has he said anything to you?"

"We did used to date, yes, but we don't talk that much now."

She studied me as she took a sip of her coffee. I took a sip as well. The flavor was a bit bitter for my taste, but it wasn't bad.

"Mmm, what brand is this?"

"It's a Colombian blend that I get sent to me. I have a friend that lives there."

"Ah, it's good."

"So, have you been able to connect with Jack or Ruben?" She looked around. "Are they here?"

"I don't see them. Let me try to connect."

I closed my eyes and pretended to focus. People assumed that's how it was done, so I sometimes played it up. The truth was the spirits were either there or they weren't. I couldn't summon them to me.

I opened my eyes to see her leaning forward, watching me with hope in her eyes. I hated to disappoint her, but they simply weren't here.

I glanced around, then admitted the truth.

"I'm sorry. They aren't here. I wish I could bring them here. I know you want to speak to them again."

"It's okay. I just wish I could have a final conversation with them." She sighed. "But I guess my last was just that."

We sat in silence for a moment. She yawned, which to me signaled my cue to leave.

"Well, I'm glad you're starting to feel better. I hope your recovery continues, but I'll let you rest."

She nodded, then walked me to the door.

"Thank you so much for coming to see me and for the plant. I have just the spot for it." She looked over her shoulder. "I don't normally keep the place so dark, but I've been resting a lot."

"I understand." I touched her arm. "Take care."

"Thanks."

We hugged, then I climbed in the car. She stood there watching me. Something felt a bit off about this whole thing, including her posture as I backed out of her driveway, but I couldn't quite explain it.

Maybe it was as simple as her not feeling well, as she'd said. Given that she'd nearly died only days before, that was a lot on a person. I know I hadn't been at my best or friendliest after my near-death experiences.

The thing that really bugged me about this whole situation was that if Jack and Ruben were her father figures and they were so close, why weren't they here? Why weren't they coming around her?

Unless they showed up again, I might never find out. They were the most hands-off ghosts I'd ever worked with. It was frustrating.

Most of my spirits had been in my face, checking in with me all the time, or at least it felt like that. Especially Jeremy Landon, who'd been the first since gaining my powers back.

I often found him sitting by my bed, startling me awake. I sure wished I'd see him again. I hadn't seen him since I adopted one of his daughters.

"She's doing well, Jeremy," I said, looking around, hoping to see his arrogant smile as he materialized.

Nothing.

That was disappointing. I wanted to tell him all about Oakley and let him know she was doing well. Perhaps he knew and was finally resting in his afterlife, no longer unhappy with his death.

I hadn't mastered the summoning ghosts piece of this yet. If I could, I'd try that with Jack and Ruben.

"Come on, guys, please let me know the truth about Kelli. About all the women."

Still nothing.

I'd just keep doing what I was doing and hoping for the best. It was clear that someone was up to no good at Birdsong, but we needed to find out who before anyone else was hurt.

Chapter Twenty-Four

I walked my last client of the day out to reception. Today felt busier than normal, but I knew it wasn't. It must just be the emotions of the Birdsong case and the sentiment of the client stories today.

They were all sad and depressing. Loved ones gone too soon, too young. Or sudden deaths in car accidents. I knew that pain.

The families were distraught, angry, and grieving. As an empathic person, I felt it along with them.

But it wasn't all doom and gloom. They all walked out with smiles on their faces and grateful words of thanks after spending a few precious moments with their loved ones. That's why I did it. Bringing them closure, final conversations, and love.

"Thank you again, Joanna." The family called out as I stood there daydreaming.

"Of course. My pleasure." I smiled, then turned to head back to my office.

First, I went to the reading room to clean up after the last appointment. We had a cleaning service that came in a few times a week, but I liked to keep things neat and tidy, especially this room since it was one of the few the clients spent time in.

After I was satisfied with the room, I went to my office to do a final check of my emails. Nothing that couldn't wait until tomorrow. My cell phone rang. Clint.

"Hey, Clint." My stomach fluttered.

"Hi, Jo," came his deep, soothing voice over the line. "I wanted to see if you had time for that coffee we keep talking about, or maybe even dinner tonight. My treat."

I checked the time. "I don't know. Janie can't stay with Oakley past five today, so I need to get home."

"Bring her. I'd love to see her too."

I hesitated only a moment. "Sure. Yes. Sounds good."

"Great. I'll pick you up at six?"

"That will work."

I'd have to give Oakley her dinner before we left, then she could snack on something from my plate at the restaurant. That way she wouldn't be cranky.

"See you then."

I stared down at my phone after we hung up. My stomach did another somersault as I thought about the pending date in just two hours. We needed to do this to either get back on track or have closure from our relationship.

But what if he asked me about marriage again? Was I ready for that? That was truly the bottom line. Could I picture being married to Clint?

The sound of someone clearing their throat broke the spell.

"Must've been some phone call, boss." Micah chuckled.

"Oh, yeah. Busted me daydreaming a bit. It was Clint asking me to dinner."

"That's progress for you both, right?"

"Maybe." I sighed. "I know he probably wants to talk about his proposal, but I don't know what to say."

"You say yes. You know you want to."

"Do I though?"

"Why wouldn't you?"

"We barely know each other. And look at Ted. I thought I knew him so well, and bam, a huge secret that got him killed."

Micah laughed a little too hard at that. "You can't base Hartley on Ted. Completely different people, boss. You know Clint is good people. He cares for you and Oakley, and even your stinky mutt."

"Hey, Chewy doesn't stink. Well, not much."

We laughed.

"But seriously, Clint is a good guy, and I think you simply panicked. Both of you need to get out of your heads and embrace love."

"Like you and Josh?"

He smiled, then frowned. "If you do get married, I recommend eloping, though. Planning a big wedding is a huge pain! Of course, doing this destination one to that resort island has made it much easier."

"I can't wait."

"Me neither." His face softened, and he exhaled slowly. "I'm complaining a bit, but I love him and can't wait for us to be legally married. Then we can start a little family."

I smiled at my longtime friend. He was so dear to me and had been by my side through a lot. I couldn't wait to see him as a father. He'd be loving and fun, strict but fair.

"You'll make a great father."

"Aw, you're sweet." He beamed. "Well, anyway, I was just checking to see when you were walking out. Tessa is closing up now, and Percy will be doing the final security check shortly."

"Oh, yes, let me just grab my stuff now."

He nodded and turned back to the hallway, leaving me.

Luckily, I'd already shut down my computer, so it was just a matter of grabbing my cell phone from the desktop and my purse from the desk drawer. I double-checked for my keys, then switched off my office light as I walked out.

I joined the rest of the employees in the reception area. We said our goodbyes and drove off towards our respective homes.

I switched on the latest audiobook I was listening to and tried not to think about Clint or marriage or the butterflies multiplying in my stomach. There really was no point since I had no idea what his side of things was.

For all I knew, he'd given up on us, or at least the getting-married part. After all, it had been weeks since he'd asked me.

As I was lost in thought, I wasn't paying attention to the surrounding cars until one bumped me from behind.

"What the...?" I looked in the rearview mirror.

The car was backing up a bit, then roared forward, hitting me again.

"Crappity, crap!"

I hit the button for Clint as I sped up and maneuvered away from the car.

"Hey, Jo. You already miss me." His voice teased.

"Clint, no, a car just rammed into me." The panic in my voice startled even me.

"Where are you?"

"On Oakhurst, just past the grocery store."

The car hit me again.

"Was that the car again?"

"Yes! I'm trying to get away, but it keeps catching up." I turned hard at the next corner, then turned again, trying to cut through the parking lot to get back to Oakhurst going the other direction. "I turned back up Oakhurst, heading towards the police station now."

"Okay, I'm heading to my truck, and I'll try to meet you along the way."

"Can you stay on the phone with me?"

"Of course. Let me just tell Terry." I heard him mumbling, then Terry's voice. "Okay, we're both on our way. I'll be in my truck and Terry in his car."

"Okay."

He talked to me as he made his way toward me.

"I don't see you yet."

The car roared up towards me, so I changed lanes, but there was a car I didn't see, so I had to swerve back. Instead, I overcorrected, and the mystery car hit me. Both actions caused me to lose complete control. I let out a string of curses as my car flipped and spun.

I remember nothing else until I woke up in the back of a moving ambulance with Clint holding my hand and two EMTs talking over me.

Panic bubbled inside me when I realized I couldn't move. I quickly took in the scene around me.

I was strapped to a stretcher with my neck immobilized. There was a blood pressure cuff strapped to one arm and another gadget on a finger. I think it measured my pulse or something.

As my senses came into focus, the panic subsided a bit. I was injured but safe with Clint. Injured might be an understatement.

"Oh, Jo, you're awake. How do you feel?" Clint asked softly.

"Like I had a car dropped on me." I tried to joke, but everything hurt. "What happened?"

I had only a fuzzy recollection, but it felt like a bad dream.

"The car caused you to wreck, but we got you now. You'll be fine." He squeezed my hand, then brought it to his lips for a gentle kiss.

"What about the other car?"

"They took off."

"That's disappointing." I tried not to cry. I stared at the white ceiling of the ambulance as stubborn tears fell down my face. "Wait!

What about Oakley?"

"Micah and Josh have her. Micah saw the whole thing, so once he knew you were being taken care of, he went to get her from Janie for you."

"And Chewy?"

"I'm sure they grabbed him too, but I'll double-check once we get settled at the hospital. Now just relax and try not to move."

The EMTs started asking me questions, but I couldn't answer them all. I tried to focus on what they were asking me, but suddenly everything started to get hazy again and the color started to drain from the world before it all went dark.

The next time I woke up, I was in the hospital still attached to a stretcher, but this one was heading into a CAT scan machine. I guess I startled the technician by looking up at her. She yelped and jumped back.

"I'm so sorry. That wasn't professional of me." She nervously laughed. "I'm Linh. We're taking a few scans."

"Concussion?"

"Probably, but we need to make sure. Also, looking for internal bleeding or broken bones, anything you could have damaged during the accident." She smiled sweetly. Her almond-shaped eyes were friendly, and her voice had a calming effect. "They have you restrained pretty well, but please try to be still. We just want to get one more image."

She walked out of my line of vision, so I couldn't see if she left the room or was doing something else. Either was possible since I couldn't see anything. It was mildly frustrating, and all I could think about was who had done this. Why had they wrecked me? And how was I in this position while they were able to drive away?

It had to be tied to the murders at Birdsong, but I hadn't recognized the car. Plus, most of the suspects didn't drive any longer. I guess if they still had a driver's license, they could rent a car.

The machine whirled to life. I was brought into the machine slowly, first stopping at my head, then it moved again, doing each part of my body. Once the scan was complete, I was moved back out. I stared at the beige ceiling and tried to remain calm, but I wanted to scream out my frustration and pain.

"Okay, that's all we need." Linh said from my right side, but still out of my line of vision.

"Now what happens?"

"We'll get you moved back to this bed, and you'll be taken to the ICU."

That's when I saw the other person in the room. She was twice the size of tiny Linh and could probably easily move me. Linh looked to be barely ninety pounds and not quite five feet tall, so how exactly was this going to work? Could she actually move me?

But looks were deceiving because on a count of three, they both lifted me, still attached to the board, onto a hospital bed.

"Now, Jade will push you to your room." Linh smiled brightly where I could see her. "I hope you feel better soon. By the way, I have your book. I love it."

"Oh, thanks." What else could I say to that?

Jade was silent as she pushed me through the hallways, then into a large elevator. I heard voices but couldn't tell how many other people were in here with us. I was in too much pain to be embarrassed, but I was angry about this whole thing.

I'd been followed, rammed, wrecked, and the idiot who did it got away. I had no idea what injuries I had or how long I'd be down from this. I had a baby and a job, plus I was supposed to have a date tonight.

Our date. I wanted to have that moment so badly, and it was stolen from me. We'd been fighting it for weeks, and it was ripped from us.

The tears started to flow slowly down my face. Jade lightly touched my hand, offering a sympathetic smile, but didn't speak. The elevator doors opened, and she pushed me out, then down what felt like a never-ending hallway. Finally, she spoke.

"Here we are, ma'am. This is a private room, so it's all you." She started hooking up monitors and an IV bag to the one in my hand that I hadn't realized was there, plus a catheter that I didn't realize was there either, but it answered one question about how I'd relieve myself. "Your family is here, and when you're ready, I can let two in at a time."

"Do you know who's here?"

"That sexy detective, your parents, sister, plus a lot of other men. I dated one of them once." She winked. "Al Washington."

I tried to hide my surprise, but I had so many questions. For now, I'd table those.

"Can you send in my sister and Al?"

"I thought you might say that." I heard her footsteps start to move away.

"Jade?"

"Yes, dear."

"How did you know I'd ask for them first?"

"Oh, I remember when Al got shot, and you were here with him. It was shortly after that when I started dating him briefly. I know you two are good friends."

"Oh, yes, you were his nurse. He's a good guy."

"He really is. I just wasn't ready for... well, I regret it a bit since."

"There's still time."

"Look at you, girl. All caring about me." She stepped closer. "I've always been a huge fan of yours."

"Thank you."

"Well, let me get your sister and Al. The others won't like it, but them's the rules."

I heard her footsteps leave the room, and what was left behind was the low hum of the machines and the muffled sounds from the hallway.

"Jo! Oh my gosh, Jo." Audrey came rushing to my side. I still couldn't turn my head yet.

Al stepped from behind her to a spot where I could see him. His face was etched with worry lines, not the usual stoic face of my dear friend.

"I'm okay. I'm okay." I whispered as Audrey buried her face into my chest. It hurt like hell, but I tried not to yelp.

"I was so scared when Clint called us." She stood back up, tears streaming down her face.

"How is Mom handling it?"

Audrey gave a half sob, half laugh. "I'm sure she'll have the doctors convinced that she needs to be admitted soon."

"Sounds right." I looked up at Al. I reached out a hand to him. "Thanks for coming."

He started to speak, but his voice cracked, so he simply

nodded. Big, strong man is also mister sensitive, and that's why I love him.

"So, besides Mom and Dad, who else is here?"

"Well, Hank, Eddie, a few others I don't know their names." She looked over to Al, who didn't look ready to speak. "Then Clint, Tessa, and Miss Ruby. Laney can't get here now because of Aspen, but she sends you love and prayers."

"Aw. As soon as I'm able, I'll text her, and of course, Micah and Josh."

"I'm going to pick up Oakley and Chewy from them after I leave here, and of course, give them an update."

"Thank you so much for that."

"Not a problem at all. We love having her and Chewy." She smiled, then looked at Al. "Well, we'd better go back and send Mom and Dad in here next, or else she'll have my head." Audrey kissed my head softly. "Love you, sis."

"Love you, sis." Then I smiled at my friend. "Al, thank you."

He smiled and kissed my head as well, then followed Audrey out.

I went through all the visitors until I'd thanked everyone. I was exhausted and seeing little cartoon birds around my head. Clint was the last visitor.

"I'm sorry we missed our date." He softly chuckled as he stroked my hand.

"Me too."

"I'm more sorry that I didn't get to you in time." His voice cracked.

"There's nothing to be sorry about. It was only the fault of the person who did it."

"I know, but..."

"I'm alive, and as soon as the doctors review the CAT scan, we'll know more."

Jade stepped into the room. "It's time that Ms. Joanna rests."

He nodded to her, then looked at me. "I'll check on you later or tomorrow. Okay?"

"Thanks."

With all my visitors gone, I settled in for a painful night in the hospital, which would have been restless too if it wasn't for all the pain medicine causing me to sleep. This was not how I thought this night would go.

A few tears slid down my face at the thought of Oakley. We wouldn't have our nighttime routine. Oh, how I enjoyed snuggles while I read to her before she went down in her crib. She'd look up with her sleepy smile and whisper that she loved me.

That was my last thought before the drugs dragged me to sleep.

Chapter Twenty-Five

~ Clint ~

I paced back and forth in the waiting room of the hospital. I couldn't believe what I'd witnessed. Joanna's car had been run off the road. It flipped and spun like you see in action movies, but this was no movie. This was real life.

My heart stopped at the sight.

As I paced, it replayed over and over in my mind. I shook my head, trying to clear the memory, but it would start all over again.

The doctors said she should make a full recovery, though it was going to be a long road. If she'd let me, I had every intention of being right there with her. But first, I had to get to the bottom of who did this to her and who was killing people at Birdsong.

Terry walked in, his expression unreadable. A trait he'd gotten good at while doing police work.

"Nothing yet on the other car. We're trying to get video footage from the nearby buildings. Hank is involved, so you know Hacker will get something for us."

"It's just frustrating. That car was drivable somehow, and Jo's here." I dropped into a nearby chair, burying my face in my hands. "It's not fair."

My friend and partner sat next to me, then put a hand on my shoulder. It wasn't much, but it was enough to comfort me. Grounding me in the moment. It stopped the scene from playing, at least for a moment.

We sat in silence for an hour until her family arrived. First was actually Hank, Al, and several of his crew. Then Joanna's brother-in-law Stan and her sister, Audrey, followed soon after by her parents. Tessa and her mother arrived next, then an aunt of Joanna's that I'd only met once before.

We gave them the last update we had, then we all waited.

I stood again, giving my seat to her family, and began to pace. Hank followed me.

"Detective, how did this happen?"

"She called me that she was being followed. I got there as fast as I could." My throat tightened as the images ran through my mind again. The moment she lost control had me nearly losing mine. I wanted to cry or punch something. "I got close when she lost control, and then the car hit her."

"No, I mean, how does this keep happening to her?"

"We don't have answers yet, but I'm hoping between what our team gathers and what Hacker can come up with, we will know."

He pointed a finger at me. "You have one job to protect her, and you've failed over and over. I have men that could do a better job, but she loves you, so do better."

He turned back towards the group, and when he sat, he put a hand on Babs' shoulder.

I was left standing there speechless. He wasn't completely wrong, but I wasn't just supposed to protect her. I had the entire town to think about, and I was trying. But I was one person in a city of over 200,000 people.

The guilt was already eating me up. Maybe I should just turn in my badge. But darn it, I wasn't a bad detective or a bad cop. There were just cases that were tougher.

I stood there for ten minutes or so, beating myself up, stewing in my guilt and anger. I wanted answers and someone's head. Figuratively, of course.

Finally, a nurse came asking for Audrey and Al. Joanna was awake and wanted them first.

"What about me? I'm her mother." Babs stomped her foot.

"She can only have two visitors at a time. She asked for her sister and Al first." The nurse crossed her arms and stared dead-eyed at her.

"Well, I don't care about that. She's my daughter, and I want to see her." Babs tried again, but Charlie put his arm gently on hers, holding her back. "But Charlie..."

"Let them go. You'll get your turn." He said sweetly as he wrapped his wife in his arms and pulled her into his chest.

I turned back towards the window and stared at the traffic moving outside, giving them peace in their private moment. My mind went back to Joanna and how I missed our few tender moments. Even though we weren't currently at that point, I still wanted to feel her against me.

I stood there in my bubble of emotions until it was my turn to see her. I was the last as everyone went before me, and rightly so. Her family was more important.

I stepped into the dark room. They had her head stabilized, so she couldn't turn to look at me. It was oddly comforting that I could take in the scene before she could see my expression.

We kept our conversation short, and her extremely protective nurse made sure it was. Joanna needed rest more than anything right now, but I just needed her to be okay.

I walked back to the waiting room where only Terry waited.

"She okay? I mean, considering." He asked.

I nodded, not trusting my voice.

"Team called. They have the video and already sent some screenshots of the car to the media."

"Good. Let's get back and see what they've got."

I looked over my shoulder towards the secured door that led back to Joanna. I wasn't a very religious person, but I said a little prayer for her before following Terry out.

Arriving at the station, we immediately went to review the video and pictures. We were disappointed, to say the least.

"All of these are too far away." I slammed my hand down on my desk.

"Yeah, no license plate either. Just a paper plate."

"I guess they did send the best of the worst to the stations." I grumbled as I continued to flip through them.

"I just hope this is enough for someone to identify the car."

My phone rang.

"Hartley," I answered.

"You have a visitor. Says his name is Hacker." It was our station's front desk.

"Walden and I will be right there. Thanks, Willis."

We moved through the bustling station to greet our guest, and I hoped he had better footage. He had a special way of getting shots.

"Hacker." Terry greeted him, then nodded for him to follow us.

Hacker followed us. The mood was somber as we trekked back to the conference room we were using. We had a whiteboard with various notes, suspects, and scenarios on it. Mostly it was a bunch of dead ends.

"So, what did you get?"

"Unfortunately, not much. I saw the pictures y'all shared with the media, and mine aren't much better."

He passed me a USB drive. I plugged it into the conference room computer, then projected it on the room's screen.

"Okay, click that folder." He pointed.

It opened to reveal a mix of still pictures and videos.

"Where should I start?" I asked.

"Try that one." He pointed to the first picture. I clicked. "See? The angle is wrong, and you can't see in the window at all."

"Yeah, can't tell if it's a male or female driver. No way to tell." I clicked to the next picture. About the same quality.

"There's no way that this person was smart enough to pull this off in just this exact spot where the cameras were just off a bit." Terry said.

"We just got unlucky." The urge to curse or punch something was back, but instead, I counted to ten twice and once in Spanish.

"I tried my best to get into all the systems I could."

I knew he had access to cameras we couldn't access. They were Hank's that were on buildings he owned, which was a good third of the town. He also had another special skill which had earned him his nickname.

"That's okay. I think this is the best we can get."

"Yeah, let's hope it's enough." Terry added, but his tone said he didn't believe it was enough any more than I did.

"This copy is for y'all. We have our own. Hank has all hands on this one. We're shaking all the trees for information."

"Thanks." After the tongue-lashing he gave me at the hospital, I wasn't surprised to hear that Hank was doing his own investigation. Perhaps his resources would find something.

Terry walked him out, and I sat there going through the files, trying to blow them up the best I could. Paper tags, dark windows with a glare in just the right spot.

Damn, damn, damn, I thought, plus a few extra curse words.

I knew this had to be related to the Birdsong murders and that we must be getting close to the killer. Things usually got more violent around Joanna right before the murderer came forward.

I stood, going to the board. I wrote "paper tags" and

"damaged car," then stepped back to read the other things on it.

Birdsong, nicotine, Phyllis, Odette, Robin, Dawn. Poisoning had a question mark next to it because we didn't have the type yet.

As if reading my mind, there was a knock at the open door, and Dr. Starke was standing there.

"Oh, hey, you must have something good if you've come here in person."

"Yeah. I got the preliminary results back from Harper's autopsy and the poisonings." He stepped in, handing me a file. "Are you ready? Nicotine."

"Seriously?" I opened the file and flipped through, reading as fast as possible. "Damn. What about the oxygen machine?"

"My guess, it was rigged to look like it was the cause. There was nothing wrong with it."

Terry walked in. "Doc, what's up?"

I handed him the file, but nobody spoke while he read it all.

"Well, crap. Now what?" He looked at me.

"Back to Birdsong. We still have Harper's apartment sealed."

"Let's go."

"Thanks, Doc." I grabbed my notepad and followed my partner out.

I didn't know if we'd find anything, but it was at least another clue to follow, and with each new piece of evidence, I felt we were getting closer.

Chapter Twenty-Six

It had been a week since my accident. Per the doctor's orders, I was taking time off from work to recover. He wanted at least two weeks off at minimum, then in two weeks I'd have a follow-up.

"Especially given your line of work." He'd beamed. I'd done a reading for him during my appointment. "I'm sure having the extra stimulus of the ghosts would make it hard to rest."

He wasn't wrong. I'd had to ask the ones that usually followed me to visit me in a few weeks. They'd all been respectful and left.

As I padded around my house now, it was empty except for my mutt and my sleeping daughter. Audrey was going to come pick her up later and entertain her for the day so I could rest.

"It'll be like when Aunt Susie used to take us, except Oakley has cousins to play with," Audrey had said when we made the plans.

"Oh, I loved our days with Aunt Susie."

I packed her bag and got it ready for a day of fun.

Between my family and friends, all my chores around the house were done, so I didn't know how I was going to keep myself busy for the day. My full instructions were low light, no screen time, and no exercise. Rest and hydrate, no sudden movement of the head and neck.

Thankfully, Chewy was easy to care for and would sleep most of the day, which was likely what I'd do as well. I took my coffee to the patio and stood there watching my favorite mutt sniff around. He ensured nothing was left unchecked.

"Ma. Ma!"

I heard Oakley call out from her room. I turned back into the house, depositing my mug on the counter before going to get her up.

"There's my sweet girl. How did you sleep?"

"No sleep."

"Right. You're awake now."

I lifted her, setting her on the floor for ease. I used to use her changing table, but she'd gotten too big for it. Jeremy and Cate were both tall people, so Oakley would likely tower over me one day.

"Do you want to wear your panda shirt?" I held it up.

"Bear." She snatched it with a giggle and tried to put it on herself.

It wouldn't be long before she could probably dress herself. The thought made me a little sad, so for now I cherished these little moments.

"Here. Let me help you." I put it on straighter so all she had to do was pull down.

When her head popped up, her whole face lit up with a bright smile. "Ta-da!"

"Yes, you did it."

I then helped her into a pair of denim shorts, a pair of pink socks, and her favorite little sneakers. I tried in vain to tame her wavy bed head. It didn't work well, and she hated when I put it in a tiny ponytail or pigtails. She'd just yank it out within ten seconds, so for today we were going wild.

"Ready to eat?"

"Yeth!" She nearly sprinted out of her room.

I was much slower on the uptake, so it took me a moment to stand. My head spun just slightly as I did, but it went away quickly.

When I arrived steps behind her in the kitchen, she was trying to jump towards the cabinets where I kept her cereal.

"Not too much longer, and you'll reach it."

I got down her box, which won me some cheers. Then I got her seated at the table. She preferred one of the regular chairs over her highchair these days. I wasn't in the mood for a battle, so I let it happen. I put a few pieces in her bowl, then got her sippy cup of milk.

"There you go. Breakfast for a champ."

"Tank."

Chewy came in from outside and wagged his tail, which won him a piece of cereal and a head pat. He wasn't a dummy. He knew where to get the good stuff.

My phone rang. Audrey.

"Are you here already?"

"No, but I'm heading out now. Just wanted to see if there was anything I could bring you or that you needed before I head over."

I looked around. She'd stocked me up on food, mostly prepared meals that she'd made. Heat and eat would be the menu choice for the next few weeks.

"There really isn't anything. You've already done so much for me."

"You sure?"

"Oh yeah."

"Great, see you shortly then."

I refilled Oakley's bowl and watched as she continued the two-for-her, one-for-Chewy method of eating.

"Done."

She held up her hands when she was finished. It was something I did to let Chewy know I was done eating. She learned so fast.

She climbed out of the chair and headed straight for a basket of tennis balls so she and her best friend could play. I had a small wash of dizziness again watching them play. It was the sudden movements that were getting me.

I'd wanted to fight Audrey a little on taking her because I'd already not seen her much. But I knew it was the right decision.

There was a knock at the door, and then in walked my sister.

"Drey!" Oakley screamed and ran to her.

It really made me miss my Aunt Susie. That was the kind of relationship we'd had with her as children. She was traveling a lot now, so we only saw her a few times a year at best. I needed to call her more.

"There's my favorite girl." She scooped up her niece, kissing her head. Chewy was just as excited to see her. He spun and barked around. "And you're always my favorite good boy."

"Thank you for taking her. She'll have so much fun." I came over and kissed my daughter's cheek, then handed my sister the bag.

"Not a problem. Are you sure you don't want me to take him too?"

We both looked down at Chewy. He'd flopped over and was on his back, tongue hanging out, smiling his big goofy grin.

I laughed at my goofy boy.

"Nah, I think we'll just sleep most of the day."

"You feeling okay?"

"A tiny bit of dizziness, but overall, much better and feeling more clearheaded each day."

My sister gave me a hug. "Please take care. I only have one sister."

"I will."

I watched them leave, then walked around my now nearly empty house. I picked up the ball they'd been playing with, dropping it back in the dog toy box.

"Now what do we do?" I asked Chewy. He wagged his tail, then went to his favorite spot in the living room to sleep. "Sounds good."

I took a spot on the couch, pulling my favorite blanket around me.

I woke up to a knock at the front door and Chewy barking. I was disoriented slightly from my nap, and I stumbled towards the door.

Peeking out, I saw Kelli from Birdsong. Chewy was sniffing the air, then made a slight growling sound. That was strange, but he hadn't met her yet, so maybe that's why.

"Hey, Kelli. What are you doing here?"

"Hi, I heard you'd been in an accident, and I just wanted to check on our favorite guest speaker at Birdsong." She handed me a small plant similar to the one I'd given her a little over a week ago. "The one you brought me brightened my day, so I thought I'd return the favor."

"Why, thank you."

We stood there in an awkward silence for a moment while my dog made a sound I hadn't heard him make before.

Was he growling?

"Would you like to come in?"

Her eyes darted to Chewy. He looked at me, then back at her. His posture was tense, and his tail was completely still. Odd.

"He's friendly." I said. "Chewy, go lay down."

He hesitated a moment, then did as he was told. Kelli seemed pleased with that and stepped inside.

"Oh, your home is lovely. I love these old craftsman-style houses. So much character."

"Me too. Not many of them left. People keep replacing them with the new modern homes."

"Nothing is sacred anymore." She laughed.

"Would you like a drink? I have water, juice, coffee, or hot tea?"

I checked the time. Still too early to offer wine or a beer. Did I even have either at the moment? I couldn't remember.

"Just water. Thank you."

I gestured for her to have a seat. "Sorry about the blanket. I was trying to follow doctor's orders."

"No worries. I understand. I was just cleared by my doctor to resume normal activity."

"Yes, of course. How are you feeling now?"

"Better. So much better."

"That was a scary incident." I said from the kitchen. "I haven't heard, did they ever figure out who did it?"

"Not that I've been told, but then the police aren't exactly open about those things. Though I heard that Phyllis was still a top suspect."

I brought over two glasses of ice water, setting one in front of Kelli.

"I hate that all of that happened. It seemed like such a quiet place."

"It was, but lately, so much drama."

Chewy picked that time to run up to me, pawing and frantic. "Do you need to go out?"

He continued pawing at me. I stood and went to open the door, but he didn't follow me. He stayed between me and Kelli.

"I'm sorry," I said to her as I came back into the living room. "He never acts like this."

"Oh, it's okay. I love dogs." She went to pet him, and he backed away with a bark.

"Chewy, that's enough."

I sat down, hoping it would calm him as I tried to smile reassuringly to Kelli. I picked up my cup to take a sip. Instead, Chewy lunged, knocking it out of my hand. All the water flew through the air, landing all over Kelli.

She jumped up with a squeal.

"Oh my gosh, oh my gosh. I'm so sorry. Let me grab a towel." I grabbed Chewy's collar and pulled him away, then pushed him into the yard. I fumbled through a kitchen drawer for a towel, then handed it to my wet guest. "I am so sorry. I don't know what's gotten into him today."

"It's okay. It happens."

But her eyes held a slight hardness that I could understand. It wasn't every day that a dog dumps water on you after growling. He made his thoughts on her known as he barked from the backyard.

"Well, I'd better get going. I'm glad you're on the mend." She looked over her shoulder towards the mess, then her eyes went towards the back door. Her gaze sent a chill up my spine. What was she thinking?

"Thank you, and I'm so glad you're doing better as well." I walked her to the door, shutting and locking it behind her. Then I peeked out the side window as she walked to her car.

She looked at my house. I hoped she couldn't see me peeking out. I wasn't good at lip reading, but I think she cursed as she climbed into her car.

After she pulled away, I turned back towards the mess. I grabbed another towel and sopped up the water from the floor, table, and couch before letting Chewy back in. He ran straight to the front door, then back to the couch. He pawed at the couch.

A small plastic vial rolled out from under the couch.

"What the heck is this?"

Not wanting him or Oakley to get it, I threw it out.

I took the wet towels to the laundry and started them.

That was a strange visit. Had I even told her where I lived? That's when my brain kicked in. I ran to the trash can and pulled out the vial.

It had a slight fishy smell. Not awful, but I knew immediately I needed to call Clint.

Chapter Twenty-Seven

~ Joanna ~

I got Clint's voicemail. I took a deep breath as I waited for the tone.

"Hey, Clint. Not sure if this is something or not, but Kelli was here. The one from Birdsong." I looked down at Chewy. "Chewy didn't like her, which is weird for him. Then after she left, I found an empty vial of... I don't know what. Just call me when you get this."

I hung up and stared at the phone. Was I being overly paranoid? I flipped the container over and over in my hand.

This could have been there for a while, from someone or something else. I racked my brain trying to think if it was from one of Oakley's toys, or was it some old makeup?

Did Janie have something here? Yeah, that could be it. I picked up my phone, opened my camera to take a picture. I then sent off a text message to her.

Her response was nearly instant.

Not mine. Haven't seen it before

Thanks

Why?

Oh, no reason. Just making sure before I throw it out.

Hopefully that didn't raise her eyebrows too much since I didn't even know if this was anything yet. I started pacing, which got Chewy's attention. He whimpered at my feet. I scratched his head.

"Do you know what this is?" He jumped at it and growled. "Is it Kelli's?"

His reaction was the same. I let out a curse and tried Clint again, then Terry. Neither of them answered. Were they on a call?

I then called my parents.

"Pick up, pick up."

No answer. Why was nobody answering? I couldn't call Audrey since she had Oakley. No reason to worry her if this was just my overactive imagination.

I turned the vial in my hand once more, then looked at my phone. I wasn't supposed to drive, but I had to go check on my parents. No matter what this was, I had to make sure they were safe.

I ran to my room and threw on some clothes, then grabbed

161

my purse and keys before sprinting out the door. I ignored the new wave of dizziness in my head.

"This is a bad idea." I looked at my phone once more before I put the car in drive.

I drove as carefully as I could. My head was not ready for this. I could have called again, but I just had to get my eyes on them.

"This is stupid. This is stupid."

Traffic was heavy, so I just took my time and was careful not to whip my head around too much. It took me longer than the normal fifteen minutes to get there, but I pulled up to Birdsong. Nothing looked crazy. No police or ambulance, so hopefully I'd gotten here before anything happened. Though I could be just freaking out for nothing.

My heart quickened as I drove around to the keypad. I typed in the code, then waited for the gate to open.

"Error?" I read the keypad message. I tried again, slowly and carefully. "Again! What the heck?"

Was my brain not working? I tried once more.

"4... 6... 6... 2." I mouthed along as I pushed the code. "Shit."

I hit the steering wheel. My stomach flopped. I had a feeling I was right about Kelli. I turned into the visitor lot and found a spot. I tried to keep my pace steady as I walked to the office.

"Hey, Velda. My code didn't work."

"That's weird. Let me check." She set down her sandwich and started to stand.

"No need right now. I'm going to check on my parents. I'll be back, and we can figure it out." I tried to give a confident, nothing-is-wrong smile. "Finish your lunch."

"Alright. Tell Babs and Charlie hi from me." She smiled and got back to her lunch.

It was on the tip of my tongue to ask if she'd seen Kelli. I didn't have a good reason to see her, and if she hadn't come in yet, I didn't want Velda to say I was looking for her. Better to just keep it to my parents.

I kept my pace normal, or as normal as possible with my head spinning and hurting all over. My recovery was going to take a step back after this expedition, and it would be for nothing if there wasn't danger on the other end of this walk.

"Hey, Joanna!"

A few residents called as I walked through. I smiled and greeted them all. My parents were several units away, roughly a five-minute walk. I passed the craft room and Kelli's office. Both were empty.

I looked around, then ducked into her office. Not sure what I was looking for, but anything that would tell me I was wrong about Kelli.

I sorted through a few things on her desk. Nothing unusual. Then I opened the first top drawer. A few paperclips, a stapler, post-it notes.

"Come on. Give me something."

I decided to go straight to the bottom drawer, skipping the middle one, because that's where I would put important stuff.

Inside were pastel-colored file folders. Each one had a resident's name on it. I flipped until I found Jack's name. It was full of articles about his wealth and his will. As I knew, everything was left to Kelli. That didn't surprise me. Though the articles threw up a red flag.

I found Ruben's, and the same, but there were also bank statements showing he'd been giving her money prior to his death. I read through the other names. I noticed a few I recognized, like Velda.

"Crap. Crap." I saw bank statements for her, articles about her going back years. "Velda is rich." I mumbled. "And she's on Kelli's list of future victims."

Or at least that's what I assumed this was.

I needed to get to my parents. I shoved the files into my bag. Thankful that I'd started carrying a large hobo style recently. I could carry the kitchen sink in this thing and still have room for more.

I then got close to Phyllis' apartment. I decided to check on her first since she was right here.

Mom had mentioned she'd started staying in her apartment again, so I thought it was worth checking on her.

When I reached her apartment, I noticed the door was cracked.

"Knock, knock. Phyllis?" I said as I stepped inside.

It looked like a struggle had occurred here. Everything was trashed. I hurried through each room. They were all the same. That's when I saw blood in her bathroom.

I pulled out my phone and took pictures as quickly as I could, then dialed Clint. Voicemail again.

"Clint, I'm at Birdsong. It's Kelli. She's the killer. Get over here." I paused for only a second. "I'll call 9-1-1 too, but hurry!"

I hung up, then dialed for emergency. They answered, and I relayed that we needed police at Birdsong.

"There might be people in danger now, so please don't come in with lights and sirens. I'm going to check on my parents. It is apartment 2403, but I have to hang up now."

"No, wait. I need to stay on..."

"You don't understand. This is an active scene, and I can't have my voice tipping off the suspect. Now send police and probably an ambulance." I hung up before they could argue with me. I just hoped they didn't call me back. I clicked my phone on silent.

Also, I honestly didn't know if they could or couldn't come without sirens and lights, but I thought it was worth throwing it in there.

I shot off a text to Clint with the pictures I'd found so at least someone else had them besides me, then I sprinted towards my parents' unit. When I got close, I could hear her voice. Kelli. It was harsh, demanding. I slowed and flattened against the wall, then crept along it until I was standing outside of my parents' door. It was slightly ajar.

"Y'all thought you were so slick. You figured out that it was me, and now you'll all pay."

"Kelli, dear, I don't think you have the balls." My mom's voice sounded strong, confident.

Go, Mom, I thought.

"Don't I? I've already killed Jack, Ruben, and the Adams. Phyllis here won't last long if that head injury isn't treated, and nobody will know it wasn't you. I'll stage it to look as if y'all killed each other. Then I'll tell the police I heard you arguing that she tried to steal your husband." Kelli laughed too loudly.

"That doesn't even make sense. Think about what you're doing." Dad said. My heart thumped with relief when I knew they were both okay, at least for now.

My cell phone rang at this moment. I thought I'd put it on silent.

"Dang it."

I tried to reach it in my pocket, but I heard Kelli curse, and her footsteps stomping my way. I barely got to see the display before Kelli reached me. She grabbed me by my collar and threw me into the apartment. I crumbled onto the floor of the foyer.

Clint would be worried when I didn't answer, but at least he had everything he needed. I just hoped he got here in time.

"Well, well, well. Look who we have here."

"Oh, hey, Kelli. How's it going?" I said casually.

"It's going much better now that you're here too. I didn't get to take you out because your ugly mutt figured me out."

I gasped at her calling my boy ugly. He was the best boy and far from ugly. No, he'd never win a best of breed because he was a mix, but he was handsome.

And if I got out of this, he was getting all his favorite treats and a basket full of new toys.

"Now I can take y'all out, and nobody will be the wiser."

"You'll never get away with it."

"Oh, but I already have."

Why do villains always say that before they finalize their plan? It was almost a guarantee that they wouldn't, but I kept my mouth shut on that one.

"Jo, are you okay? How did you get here?" Mom asked when Kelli dragged me into the view of everyone else.

I took in the full scene. Phyllis was lying on the floor. I could see she was breathing, but she had an ugly gash on her forehead. The blood had dripped, but it definitely needed attention. My parents looked okay but were handcuffed together and seated on the floor.

"I drove."

"You aren't supposed to be driving. What about your concussion?" She scolded.

"A concussion is the least of her problems at this point." Kelli laughed. "She's going to die very soon."

Kelli paced, and that's when I noticed the gun shoved into the back of her pants.

"What are you waiting on?" I taunted.

"Jo!" Dad gasped. Phyllis moaned.

"If she was going to do something, she'd just do it, but I think she's waiting for something or someone."

Kelli laughed. It was like nails on a chalkboard, and I really wanted to goad her more and more. She wasn't the messy kind of killer. That's why she always poisoned her victims. She was going to use a violent death as a last resort. I just had to stall her until the cavalry got here.

Chapter Twenty-Eight

~ Clint ~

I'd worked a near twenty-four-hour shift. Not something I did often, and I was sleeping it off. When I woke, I stretched and made my way to the bathroom. Then I headed from there to the coffeepot. Yes, it was the middle of the afternoon, but I needed a pick-me-up.

With mug in hand, I backtracked to my bedroom to grab my phone. I'd left it on silent while I caught up on sleep.

"Twelve missed calls and fifteen texts." Damn it.

I punched through them, cursing a little more as I read and heard Joanna's words.

"Kelli is our killer."

I threw on clothes as I called Joanna back. It went to voicemail. That was strange. Then my blood ran cold. She was with Kelli. I knew it in a second.

I called Terry and got him heading this way, then I called dispatch.

"Yeah, we got a call to head out to Birdsong. The caller was Joanna Webber. She said no lights, no sirens. Hartley, you know we can't..."

"I know, but in this case, do it. Sirens and lights off before approaching. Now. Do it."

The dispatcher quickly typed in the order.

"How many en route?"

"One car. Two officers."

I cursed under my breath. "Get more out there. Immediately. Again, this is a quiet op."

I heard a honk outside the door. That must be Terry. I jogged out to the car and jumped in, but I stayed on the phone with our dispatcher until he confirmed that more units were dispatched to Birdsong. I'd also asked him to send a couple of ambulances since I didn't know what we were going to find, given Joanna's pictures of blood.

She hadn't given context, and there was no way of knowing if this was her blood and someone had her phone, or if she'd sent them herself.

"Alright, what's going on?"

"Joanna called, leaving me a voicemail." I played it for him. "Then she sent a bunch of pictures. I'm assuming it was her, assuming nobody stole her phone from her. I'm not sure, but this might be Phyllis King's place. I kind of remember this poster. This one is blood in the bathroom."

"Hers? Someone else's?"

"Don't know yet."

"What did dispatch say?"

"They had one unit, but I got them to send more plus a couple of EMTs."

"Good."

We drove the rest of the way in silence until the last mile or so when we got the call I'd been dreading.

"Hostage situation at Birdsong," was the message that came over our radios.

Terry looked my way as we turned up the long drive. He parked as close as he could, then we joined our fellow officers. We got a quick debrief from the scene lead, then we helped set up the perimeter.

"Who do we have to negotiate?" Terry asked.

"Morrison is heading over there now." Officer Williams said.

He was our best hostage negotiator. He was likable and calm. If anyone could get this under control, it was him. He'd only lost one out of hundreds in his thirty-year career. He'd come to Creekview about five years ago from New York City, and before that, Boston.

"Good." I nodded and made my way through the barrier to the main office. A distraught Velda greeted me.

"Oh, Detective Hartley, it's awful." She sobbed. "Kelli has been doing it all. I trusted her, loved her like a daughter."

So word had gotten out, I thought.

"Are you okay?" I asked her. I wasn't always the most empathic, but I was trying.

"No, but yes. I'm just shocked." She gestured for me to go ahead to the back door.

I touched her arm gently as I passed by, then I headed towards the Webbers' apartment. It was near the back of the community, but we had a second command center towards the middle of the residence. I wanted to touch base with Morrison and see if he'd begun discussions with Kelli.

"Hartley, hey." Morrison greeted. "This is your lady's folks, right?"

"Um, yeah, that's right."

I didn't know how much she was my lady, but I hoped if this turned out okay, I was going to correct that. I promised myself I was going to stop being a wimp about this whole thing. Life was short. Hadn't I learned that too many times? But it was made better with someone to share those days with.

"I was just about to start negotiations. Ready?" He nodded to one of the other officers standing there at the command center. I could hear the phone ringing at his ear.

"Hi, is this Kelli?" I heard a mumble through the phone as she replied, then he continued. "Well, hi, this is Officer Morrison. Can I bring you anything? Water, maybe? No, I'm not going to be armed or anything. I just want to talk and get my eyes on the victims. Yes, yes. I hear you. Why don't I bring you a bottle of water, and we can talk in person. Great. I'll see you in a minute."

"That sounds promising, yeah?" I asked when he'd hung up.

"I think so. Now I'll go in and try to talk her down and get everyone released." He offered a salute as he grabbed the bottle of water he'd offered Kelli. Then he strode across the yard and down the hallway, out of sight.

I paced a few steps around the command center as I waited for word, any word that all the Webbers were okay. My main concern was for one specifically, but the other two were just as important to me. I also knew she had Phyllis King with her. Phyllis had some kind of injury, which we'd confirmed when we'd arrived. Velda had let the first on scene know that it had been her apartment.

"Your girl is smart." Officer Williams said as she came up from behind me. "Sending you those pictures and giving the details to the 9-1-1 operator helped us be prepared."

"Yeah, except the operator didn't believe all the information."

"I've already made note of that, and there will be additional training."

I nodded. We were quiet as we waited for Morrison to report back or call for backup. Time seemed to stand still as we waited.

Williams tried to make small talk to help, but I barely heard her. Everything in my world seemed dulled and warbled at the same time. I was listening for one sound and one sound only. Gunshots. If I heard those, I'd be across this lawn in seconds.

It was easily fifteen minutes before Morrison called us on the radios. He said he had Kelli in custody and would need the EMTs to assist.

I sprinted towards the apartment. Morrison walked past me with a handcuffed Kelli. She said a curse in my direction. I let it go and continued my trek. Just as I reached their door, Joanna emerged. Her face was pale and her eyes wide, but when she saw me, her face softened, and she rushed towards me.

"Clint, I'm so happy to see you." She sobbed into my chest.

"I'm so happy to see you too. Are you okay?"

"Just a little dizzy. My concussion, but otherwise fine." She turned towards the apartment. "My folks..."

I held her from walking in. "Let me check."

I walked in to see an EMT taking Charlie's blood pressure. Babs was hovering over Phyllis as an EMT was attending to her. Otherwise, they both looked fine. I stepped back a few paces to get Joanna. I wanted her inside and sitting.

Once the EMT was finished with Charlie, I signaled for her to come check Jo.

"She had a concussion last week and really shouldn't be out like this." I then turned towards Babs and Charlie. "Are you both okay?"

"Yes, thank you, son." Charlie said, clapping me on the back before checking on his wife. She was still looking over her friend.

"Good. Good. How is she?" I nodded towards Phyllis.

"In shock a bit. She sustained a serious head injury, but I think she'll be okay." The EMT cleaning her up said.

Phyllis looked at me with glazed eyes and nodded, or tried to. It was a bit wobbly.

Relief flooded my body that all of them were okay. No additional bodies. Thank goodness.

Chapter Twenty-Nine

We were all taken to the hospital after being saved by Officer Morrison. I hadn't met him before, but I was in awe of his skills. He'd talked us all out of certain death. Even though Kelli was the type who didn't want to get her hands dirty, I could see that something in her had snapped. Today might have been that day.

I heard her explaining to Morrison why she'd done it.

"Money. I wanted the money."

"Why? Money isn't as important as friends, family."

"I don't have any family. I never did."

She explained being kicked out as a teenager and having to do whatever she could to survive. It was heartbreaking, really, but it didn't excuse what she'd done. She'd come up with this scheme when she was working at a nursing home.

"Some people don't have anyone, but they have wealth and no one to leave it to."

She said one lady was so sweet to her and Kelli had gone out of her way to be there for her. After the lady passed, leaving her everything in her will, Kelli realized she could make a living at it.

"I only stay at one place for a few years, just long enough to pad my bank account, and then I move along. This was meant to be my last place. Then I was going to retire."

"Well, that's an awful story, Kelli, but wouldn't it be better to let these people go? We can get you help."

"No, they're trying to ruin my life."

"I don't think they are. Let's end this."

There was more, but I was in and out of it. I just know it wasn't long before she surrendered. She put her hands out and he clipped handcuffs on her.

My parents were fine. A little bruised from Kelli forcing them into cuffs and hitting them around a bit. Phyllis had a concussion, but the doctors confirmed she should be okay. No other residents were harmed.

As for me, I got a lecture from the doctor who'd treated me after the car accident.

"Ms. Joanna," the doctor said, "I see you didn't follow our

orders to rest."

"Had I rested, a lot more people would be dead." I smiled sweetly.

"Touché." He smirked. "But now we'll need to do another CAT scan to see how your head is, especially after you got knocked around a bit. Overall though, you're really lucky."

I felt lucky. I hadn't been shot this time and everyone would get to go home, except for Kelli. She had a one-way ticket to jail until she stood trial.

Jade entered my room. "Well, Ms. Joanna, did you miss me already? Had to come back and see ole Jade, did ya?" She chuckled.

"Yes, of course." I laughed with her.

"Well, Doctor Cullen says overnight for you."

"No. I can't." But my spinning head told me it was the right thing to do.

"I've already talked to the sexy detective. He says he'll get your dog, and your mother confirmed that your sister is keeping the baby, so looks like you're stuck with me for the night."

I sighed and nodded slowly.

"That's better. Now, do you want some juice and water? Maybe a jello?"

"Thanks, Jade. That sounds good."

"I remember your favorites." She turned. "I'll be back in a jiffy."

I relaxed into the bed and waited, but before Jade returned, my parents came in. They both looked a few years older, likely from the worry and stress of today, but had been cleared to go home.

"I'm so glad you're okay, Jo." Dad came over to kiss my head.

"And we've talked to Audrey. She's concerned about us all but said she would keep Oakley for as long as you need."

"I'm glad you're both okay. Kelli snapped."

"It was nothing we couldn't handle." Mom laughed. "She doesn't know who she's messing with."

I didn't know who this woman before me was, but she'd changed so much over the last few weeks. I knew it was all because of Phyllis.

"How is Phyllis?"

"She's down the hall from you. She'll be staying a night or

two, but she's fine. Just banged up and a concussion, same as you."

"I'm so glad."

Jade came in with my drinks and snack. She gave my parents a pointed look, probably a two-minute warning.

"Nice to see you, Jade." Mom said sweetly. She leaned over to hug me. "We'll check on you in the morning. Rest up, Joanna."

My dad kissed my forehead and they both left.

Jade got me settled and left me alone. I sipped at my juice and slurped up my lime jello before settling into the bed for rest.

It was a few weeks later, and I was finally able to drive and go about life as normal. I was heading over with Oakley to have lunch at Birdsong.

I pulled up and punched in my code, holding my breath as I remembered the last time. This time the gate slid open without issue. I drove around, waving to a few residents as I did. I parked in the visitor spot closest to my folks.

"There are my girls!" Mom called out from her back door. She walked over to help me with the baby. "How are you feeling today?"

"Better. Much better. It felt good to drive again too."

"Gamma!" Oakley yelled and threw herself toward one of her favorite people.

I grabbed the bag and stroller, then followed mom and baby to the apartment.

"Where's dad?" I asked, realizing he wasn't home.

"Playing cards with the guys. He said he was going to leave us girls to lunch."

Just then there was a knock at the door. In walked Phyllis along with Alma Jean, Odette, Robin, and Dawn.

"Hey, ladies." Mom said. "Y'all remember my daughter and granddaughter, right?"

"Of course, hi." came a chorus from the ladies.

"Um, oh, hi. I didn't know we would have such a crowd today."

"Yeah, well, we've all kissed and made up, so to speak." Odette chuckled.

"Yes, we realized Kelli had put thoughts in our heads, and once we all talked, we realized how silly everything was." Phyllis smiled at the others.

"Oh, I'm so glad to hear it." I smiled. "Does that mean you aren't moving out?" I asked Phyllis.

"That's right. I'm here to stay."

I knew that was going to make mom happy, and I loved seeing this new side of her. The lady who'd been so overprotective and a little controlling all my life had finally found her tribe.

Oakley started entertaining the ladies. They laughed as they watched her make silly faces and dance, something she'd recently started doing.

My phone rang. Clint. My heart skipped a beat. Since seeing him the other day, I'd been optimistic about us getting back together, but I'd kept my wall up a bit.

"Would you excuse me? Oh, mom, can you watch her?"

"Of course." She winked. I guess she knew who it was.

I stepped out the back door into the parking lot and answered. "Hey."

"Hey, Jo. I just wanted to see how you were feeling."

"Better. Much better. Today was a return to driving day, so I came over to visit my parents."

"Oh, yeah? I'm here too."

"You are?"

"I had to wrap up some of our investigation. May I stop by for a second?"

"Yeah, of course."

"Turn around."

I turned slowly to find him standing with a single rose in hand. "Clint... wow." I said it into the phone, then realized my mistake. "Oh, bye." I hung up.

He laughed and stepped forward. "I know exactly where I went wrong last time. I should have talked about my feelings, not just assumed we were on the same page. Heck, we may not have even been in the same book." He stepped closer. "But please know that I will do whatever it takes to make this work between us because the last few weeks have been hell." He took another step. "What do ya say? Can we go back to being an us again?"

"Oh, Clint. Yes, that's what I want too."

He pulled me into his arms and kissed me. When we broke

apart, he rested his forehead against mine.

"I'm not letting you go this time. You're stuck with me, Joanna Webber."

"I think I can live with that."

We walked back toward the apartment hand in hand, and for the first time in weeks, everything felt right. My parents were safe and happy. My friends were reconciled. And I had Clint back.

Life was good.

Before you go: If you loved Crafted Murder and haven't already received a copy of Unsolved Murder, the prequel to this series check out my website for the offer for your free novella.

www.ejwheltonwrites.com

Author note:

I had a lot of fun writing this one. It felt like it took me forever to get it across the finish line, but I hope you agree that it was a fun read.

My own grandparents lived in a senior community and that's what inspired me to write this story. After my grandfather had passed, my grandmother would talk about all the drama. When I'd have lunch with her in the cafeteria, she would smile at some of the ladies and then whisper that they were jealous she could still drive.

There was also a Kelli that worked there. She always had fun things played for the residents. She was the sweetest person in the world and in no way would have done what fictional Kelli did, but I included her for fun.

Again, if you enjoyed this book and haven't gotten your free novella, Unsolved Murder, please be sure to stop by my website for details.

www.ejwheltonwrites.com

www.ingramcontent.com/pod-product-compliance
Lightning Source LLC
Chambersburg PA
CBHW020815190726
48285CB00006B/2287